D0258357

gossip girl

Gossip Girl novels by Cecily von Ziegesar:

Gossip Girl
You Know You Love Me

gossip girl

A Novel by

Cecily von Ziegesar

BLOOMSBURY

Published in Great Britain in 2003 by Bloomsbury Publishing Plc
38 Soho Square, London W1D 3HB

This edition published by arrangement with
Little, Brown & Company (Inc.), New York, NY, USA.
All rights reserved

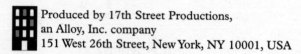

Produced by 17th Street Productions,
an Alloy, Inc. company
151 West 26th Street, New York, NY 10001, USA

Copyright © 2002 by 17th Street Productions, an Alloy, Inc. company
The moral right of the author has been asserted

All rights reserved
No part of this publication may be produced or
transmitted by any means, electronic, mechanical, photocopying or
otherwise, without the prior permission of the publisher

A CIP catalogue record of this book is available from the
British Library
ISBN 0 7475 6342 X

Printed in Great Britain by Clays Ltd, St Ives plc

10 9 8 7 6 5 4 3 2 1

"Scandal is gossip made tedious by morality."
—Oscar Wilde

gossip girl

 gossipgirl.co.uk

Disclaimer: All the real names of places, people, and events have been altered or abbreviated to protect the innocent. Namely, me.

hey people!

Ever wondered what the lives of the chosen ones are really like? Well, I'm going to tell you, because I'm one of them. I'm not talking about beautiful models or actors or musical prodigies or mathematical geniuses. I'm talking about the people who are *born to it*—those of us who have everything anyone could possibly wish for and who take it all completely for granted.

Welcome to New York City's Upper East Side, where my friends and I live and go to school and play and sleep—sometimes with each other. We all live in huge apartments with our own bedrooms and bathrooms and phone lines. We have unlimited access to money and booze and whatever else we want, and our parents are rarely home, so we have tons of privacy. We're smart, we've inherited classic good looks, we wear fantastic clothes, and we know how to party. Our shit still stinks, but you can't smell it because the bathroom is sprayed hourly by the maid with a refreshing scent made exclusively for us by French perfumers.

It's a luxe life, but someone's got to live it.

Our apartments are all within walking distance of the Metropolitan Museum of Art on Fifth Avenue, and the single-sex private schools, like Constance Billard, which most of us go to. Even with a hangover, Fifth Avenue always looks so beautiful in the morning with the sunlight glimmering on the heads of the sexy St. Jude's School boys.

But something is rotten on museum mile. . . .

SIGHTINGS

B with her mother, arguing in a taxi in front of **Takashimaya**. *N* enjoying a joint on the steps of the **Met**. *C* buying new school shoes at **Barneys**. And a familiar, tall, eerily beautiful blond girl emerging from a New Haven line train in **Grand Central Station**. Approximate age, seventeen. Could it be? *S* is back?!

THE GIRL WHO LEAVES FOR BOARDING SCHOOL, GETS KICKED OUT, AND COMES BACK

Yes, *S* is back from boarding school. Her hair is longer, paler. Her blue eyes have that deep mysteriousness of kept secrets. She is wearing the same old fabulous clothes, now in rags from fending off New England storms. This morning *S*'s laughter echoed off the steps of the Met, where we will no longer be able to enjoy a quick smoke and a cappuccino without seeing her waving to us from her parents' apartment across the street. She has picked up the habit of biting her fingernails, which makes us wonder about her even more, and while we are all dying to ask her why she got kicked out of boarding school, we won't, because we'd really rather she had stayed away. But *S* is definitely here.

Just to be safe, we should all synchronize our watches. If we aren't careful, *S* is going to win over our teachers, wear that dress we couldn't fit into, eat the last olive, have sex in our parents' beds, spill Campari on our rugs, steal our brothers' and our boyfriends' hearts, and basically ruin our lives and piss us all off in a major way.

I'll be watching closely. I'll be watching all of us. It's going to be a wild and wicked year. I can smell it.

Love,

gossip girl

like most juicy stories,
it started at a party

"I watched Nickelodeon all morning in my room so I wouldn't have to eat breakfast with them," Blair Waldorf told her two best friends and Constance Billard School classmates, Kati Farkas and Isabel Coates. "My mother cooked him an omelet. I didn't even know she knew how to use the stove."

Blair tucked her long, dark brown hair behind her ears and swigged her mother's fine vintage scotch from the crystal tumbler in her hand. She was already on her second glass.

"What shows did you watch?" Isabel asked, removing a stray strand of hair from Blair's black cashmere cardigan.

"Who cares?" Blair said, stamping her foot. She was wearing her new black ballet flats. Very bow-tie proper preppy, which she could get away with because she could change her mind in an instant and put on her trashy, pointed, knee-high boots and that sexy metallic skirt her mother hated. Poof—rock star sex kitten. Meow.

"The point is, I was trapped in my room all morning because they were busy having a gross romantic breakfast in their matching red silk bathrobes. They didn't even take *showers*." Blair took another gulp of her drink. The only way to tolerate the thought of her mother sleeping with *that man* was to get drunk—very drunk.

Luckily Blair and her friends came from the kind of families for whom drinking was as commonplace as blowing your nose. Their parents believed in the quasi-European idea that the more access kids have to alcohol, the less likely they are to abuse it. So Blair and her friends could drink whatever they wanted, whenever they wanted, as long as they maintained their grades and their looks and didn't embarrass themselves or the family by puking in public, pissing their pants, or ranting in the streets. The same thing went for everything else, like sex or drugs—as long as you kept up appearances, you were all right.

But keep your panties on. That's coming later.

The man Blair was so upset about was Cyrus Rose, her mother's new boyfriend. At that very moment Cyrus Rose was standing on the other side of the living room, greeting the dinner guests. He looked like someone who might help you pick out shoes at Saks—bald, except for a small, bushy mustache, his fat stomach barely hidden in a shiny blue double-breasted suit. He jingled the change in his pocket incessantly, and when he took his jacket off, there were big, nasty sweat marks on his underarms. He had a loud laugh and was very sweet to Blair's mother. But he wasn't Blair's father. Last year Blair's father ran off to France with another man.

No kidding. They live in a chateau and run a vineyard together. Which is actually pretty cool if you think about it.

Of course none of that was Cyrus Rose's fault, but that didn't matter to Blair. As far as Blair was concerned, Cyrus Rose was a completely annoying, fat, *loser*.

But tonight Blair was going to have to tolerate Cyrus Rose, because the dinner party her mother was giving was in his honor, and all the Waldorfs' family friends were there to meet him: the Bass family and their sons Chuck and Donald; Mr. Farkas and his daughter, Kati; the well-known actor Arthur

Coates, his wife Titi, and their daughters, Isabel, Regina, and Camilla; Captain and Mrs. Archibald and their son Nate. The only ones still missing were Mr. and Mrs. van der Woodsen whose teenage daughter, Serena, and son, Erik, were both away at school.

Blair's mother was famous for her dinner parties, and this was her first since her infamous divorce. The Waldorf penthouse had been expensively redecorated that summer in deep reds and chocolate browns, and it was full of antiques and artwork that would have impressed anyone who knew anything about art. In the center of the dining room table was an enormous silver bowl full of white orchids, pussy willows, and chestnut tree branches—a modern ensemble from Takashimaya, the Fifth Avenue luxury goods store. Gold-leafed place cards lay on every porcelain plate. In the kitchen, Myrtle the cook was singing Bob Marley songs to the soufflé, and the sloppy Irish maid, Esther, hadn't poured scotch down anyone's dress yet, thank God.

Blair was the one getting sloppy. And if Cyrus Rose didn't stop harassing Nate, her boyfriend, she was going to have to go over there and spill her scotch all over his tacky Italian loafers.

"You and Blair have been going out a long time, am I right?" Cyrus said, punching Nate in the arm. He was trying to get the kid to loosen up a little. All these Upper East Side kids were way too uptight.

That's what he thinks. Give them time.

"You sleep with her yet?" Cyrus asked.

Nate turned redder than the upholstery on the eighteenth-century French chaise next to him. "Well, we've known each other practically since we were born," he stuttered. "But we've only been going out for like, a year. We don't want to ruin it by, you know, rushing, before we're ready?" Nate was just spitting back the line that Blair always gave him when he asked her if she was ready to do it or not. But he was talking to his girl-friend's mother's boyfriend. What was he supposed to say, "Dude, if I had my way we'd be doing it right *now*"?

"Absolutely," Cyrus Rose said. He clasped Nate's shoulder with a fleshy hand. Around his wrist was one of those gold Cartier cuff bracelets that you screw on and never take off—very popular in the 1980s and not so popular now, unless you've actually bought into that whole '80s revival thing. *Hello?*

"Let me give you some advice," Cyrus told Nate, as if Nate had a choice. "Don't listen to a word that girl says. Girls like surprises. They want you to keep things interesting. You know what I mean?"

Nate nodded, frowning. He tried to remember the last time he'd surprised Blair. The only thing that came to mind was the time he'd brought her an ice cream cone when he picked her up at her tennis lesson. That was over a month ago, and it was a pretty lame surprise by any standard. At this rate, he and Blair might never have sex.

Nate was one of those boys you look at and while you're looking at them, you know they're thinking, *that girl can't take her eyes off me because I'm so hot.* Although he didn't act at all conceited about it. He couldn't help looking hot, he was just born that way. Poor guy.

That night Nate was wearing the moss-green cashmere V-neck sweater Blair had given him last Easter, when her father had taken them skiing in Sun Valley for a week. Secretly, Blair had sewn a tiny gold heart pendant onto the inside of one of the sweater's sleeves, so that Nate would always be wearing her heart on his sleeve. Blair liked to think of herself as a hopeless romantic in the style of old movie actresses like Audrey Hepburn and Marilyn Monroe. She was always coming up with plot devices for the movie she was starring in at the moment, the movie that was her life.

"I love you," Blair had told Nate breathily when she gave him the sweater.

"Me too," Nate had said back, although he wasn't exactly sure if it was true or not.

When he put the sweater on, it looked so good on him that Blair wanted to scream and rip all her clothes off. But it seemed unattractive to scream in the heat of the moment— more femme fatale than girl-who-gets-boy—so Blair kept quiet, trying to remain fragile and baby-birdlike in Nate's arms. They kissed for a long time, their cheeks hot and cold at the same time from being out on the slopes all day. Nate twined his fingers in Blair's hair and pulled her down on the hotel bed. Blair put her arms above her head and let Nate begin to undress her, until she realized where this was all heading, and that it wasn't a movie after all, it was *real*. So, like a good girl, she sat up and made Nate stop.

She'd kept on making him stop right on up until today. Only two nights ago, Nate had come over after a party with a half-drunk flask of brandy in his pocket and had lain down on her bed and murmured, "I want you, Blair." Once again, Blair had wanted to scream and jump on top of him, but she resisted. Nate fell asleep, snoring softly, and Blair lay down next to him and imagined that she and Nate were starring in a movie in which they were married and he had a drinking problem, but she would stand by him always and love him forever, even if he occasionally wet the bed.

Blair wasn't trying to be a tease, she just wasn't *ready*. She and Nate had barely seen each other at all over the summer because she had gone to that horrible boot camp of a tennis school in North Carolina, and Nate had gone sailing with his father off the coast of Maine. Blair wanted to make sure that after spending the whole summer apart they still loved each other as much as ever. She had wanted to wait to have sex until her seventeenth birthday next month.

But now she was through with waiting.

Nate was looking better than ever. The moss-green sweater had turned his eyes a dark, sparkling green, and his wavy brown hair was streaked with golden blond from his summer on the ocean. And, just like that, Blair knew she was ready. She took another sip of her scotch. *Oh, yes.* She was definitely ready.

an hour of sex burns 360 calories

"What are you two talking about?" Blair's mother asked, sidling up to Nate and squeezing Cyrus's hand.

"Sex," Cyrus said, giving her a wet kiss on the ear.

Yuck.

"Oh!" Eleanor Waldorf squealed, patting her blown-out blond bob.

Blair's mother was wearing the fitted, graphite-beaded cashmere dress that Blair had helped her pick out from Armani, and little black velvet mules. A year ago she wouldn't have fit into the dress, but she had lost twenty pounds since she met Cyrus. She looked fantastic. Everyone thought so.

"She does look thinner," Blair heard Mrs. Bass whisper to Mrs. Coates. "But I'll bet she's had a chin tuck."

"I bet you're right. She's grown her hair out—that's the telltale sign. It hides the scars," Mrs. Coates whispered back.

The room was abuzz with snatches of gossip about Blair's mother and Cyrus Rose. From what Blair could hear, her mother's friends felt exactly the same way she did, although they didn't exactly use words like annoying, fat, or loser.

"I smell Old Spice," Mrs. Coates whispered to Mrs. Archibald. "Do you think he's actually *wearing* Old Spice?"

That would be the male equivalent of wearing Impulse body spray, which everyone knows is the female equivalent of nasty.

"I'm not sure," Mrs. Archibald whispered back. "But I think he might be." She snatched a cod-and-caper spring roll off Esther's platter, popped it into her mouth, and chewed it vigorously, refusing to say anything more. She couldn't bear for Eleanor Waldorf to overhear them. Gossip and idle chat were amusing, but not at the expense of an old friend's feelings.

Bullshit! Blair would have said if she could have heard Mrs. Archibald's thoughts. *Hypocrite!* All of these people were terrible gossips. And if you're going to do it, why not enjoy it?

Across the room, Cyrus grabbed Eleanor and kissed her on the lips in full view of everyone. Blair shrank away from the revolting sight of her mother and Cyrus acting like geeky teens with a crush and turned to look out the penthouse window at Fifth Avenue and Central Park. The fall foliage was on fire. A lone bicyclist rode out of the Seventy-second Street entrance to the park and stopped at the hot-dog vendor on the corner to buy a bottle of water. Blair had never noticed the hot-dog vendor before, and she wondered if he always parked there, or if he was new. It was funny how much you could miss in what you saw every day.

Suddenly Blair was starving, and she knew just what she wanted: A hot dog. She wanted one *right now*—a steaming hot Sabrette hot dog with mustard and ketchup and onions and sauerkraut—and she was going to eat it in three bites and then burp in her mother's face. If Cyrus could stick his tongue down her mother's throat in front of all of her friends, then she could eat a stupid hot dog.

"I'll be right back," Blair told Kati and Isabel.

She whirled around and began to walk across the room to the front hall. She was going to put on her coat, go outside, get a hot dog from the vendor, eat it in three bites, come back, burp in her mother's face, have another drink, and then have sex with Nate.

"Where are you going?" Kati called after her. But Blair didn't stop; she headed straight for the door.

Nate saw Blair coming and extracted himself from Cyrus and Blair's mother just in time.

"Blair?" he said. "What's up?"

Blair stopped and looked up into Nate's sexy green eyes. They were like the emeralds in the cufflinks her father wore with his tux when he went to the opera.

He's wearing your heart on his sleeve, she reminded herself, forgetting all about the hot dog. In the movie of her life, Nate would pick her up and carry her away to the bedroom and ravish her.

But this was real life, unfortunately.

"I have to talk to you," Blair said. She held out her glass. "Fill me up, first?"

Nate took her glass and Blair led him over to the marble-topped wet bar by the French doors that opened onto the dining room. Nate poured them each a tumbler full of scotch and then followed Blair across the living room once more.

"Hey, where are you two going?" Chuck Bass asked as they walked by. He raised his eyebrows, leering at them suggestively.

Blair rolled her eyes at Chuck and kept walking, drinking as she went. Nate followed her, ignoring Chuck completely.

Chuck Bass, the oldest son of Misty and Bartholomew Bass, was handsome, aftershave-commercial handsome. In fact, he'd starred in a British Drakkar Noir commercial, much to his parents' public dismay and secret pride. Chuck was also the horniest boy in Blair and Nate's group of friends. Once, at a party in ninth grade, Chuck had hidden in a guest bedroom closet for two hours, waiting to crawl into bed with Kati Farkas, who was so drunk she kept throwing up in her sleep. Chuck didn't even mind. He just got in bed with her. He was completely unshakeable when it came to girls.

The only way to deal with a guy like Chuck is to laugh in his face, which is exactly what all the girls who knew him did. In other circles, Chuck might have been banished as a slimeball of the highest order, but these families had been friends for generations. Chuck was a Bass, and so they were stuck with him. They had even gotten used to his gold monogrammed pinky ring, his trademark navy blue monogrammed cashmere scarf, and the copies of his headshot, which littered his parent's many houses and apartments and spilled out of his locker at the Riverside Preparatory School for Boys.

"Don't forget to use protection," Chuck called, raising his glass at Blair and Nate as they turned down the long, red-carpeted hallway to Blair's bedroom.

Blair grasped the glass doorknob and turned it, surprising her Russian Blue cat, Kitty Minky, who was curled up on the red silk bedspread. Blair paused at the threshold and leaned back against Nate, pressing her body into his. She reached down to take his hand.

At that moment, Nate's hopes perked up. Blair was acting sort of sultry and sexy and could it be . . . *something was about to happen?*

Blair squeezed Nate's hand and pulled him into the room. They stumbled over each other, falling toward the bed, and spilling their drinks on the mohair rug. Blair giggled; the scotch she'd pounded had gone right to her head.

I'm about to have sex with Nate, she thought giddily. And then they'd both graduate in June and go to Yale in the fall and have a huge wedding four years later and find a beautiful apartment on Park Avenue and decorate the whole thing in velvet, silk, and fur and have sex in every room on a rotating basis.

Suddenly Blair's mother's voice rang out, loud and clear, down the hallway.

"Serena van der Woodsen! What a lovely surprise!"

Nate dropped Blair's hand and straightened up like a soldier called to attention. Blair sat down hard on the end of her bed, put her drink on the floor, and grasped the bedspread in tight, white-knuckled fists.

She looked up at Nate.

But Nate was already turning to go, striding back down the hall to see if it could possibly be true. Had Serena van der Woodsen *really* come back?

The movie of Blair's life had taken a sudden, tragic turn. Blair clutched her stomach, ravenous again.

She should have gone for the hot dog after all.

s is back!

"Hello, hello, hello!" Blair's mother crowed, kissing the smooth, hollow cheeks of each van der Woodsen.

Kiss, kiss, kiss, kiss, kiss, *kiss!*

"I know you weren't expecting Serena, dear," Mrs. van der Woodsen whispered in a concerned, confidential tone. "I hope it's all right."

"Of course. Yes, it's fine," Mrs. Waldorf said. "Did you come home for the weekend, Serena?"

Serena van der Woodsen shook her head and handed her vintage Burberry coat to Esther, the maid. She pushed a stray blond hair behind her ear and smiled at her hostess.

When Serena smiled, she used her eyes—those dark, almost navy blue eyes. It was the kind of smile you might try to imitate, posing in the bathroom mirror like an idiot. The magnetic, delicious, "you can't stop looking at me, can you?" smile supermodels spend years perfecting. Well, Serena smiled that way without even trying.

"No, I'm here to—" Serena started to say.

Serena's mother interrupted hastily. "Serena has decided that boarding school is not for her," she announced, patting her hair casually, as if it were no big deal. She was the middle-aged version of utter coolness.

The whole van der Woodsen family was like that. They were all tall, blond, thin, and super-poised, and they never did anything—play tennis, hail a cab, eat spaghetti, go to the toilet—without maintaining their cool. Serena especially. She was gifted with the kind of coolness that you can't acquire by buying the right handbag or the right pair of jeans. She was the girl every boy wants and every girl wants to be.

"Serena will be back at Constance tomorrow," Mr. van der Woodsen said, glancing at his daughter with steely blue eyes and an owl-like mixture of pride and disapproval that made him look scarier than he really was.

"Well, Serena. You look lovely, dear. Blair will be thrilled to see you," Blair's mother trilled.

"You're one to talk," Serena said, hugging her. "Look how skinny you are! And the house looks so fantastic. Wow. You've got some awesome art!"

Mrs. Waldorf smiled, obviously pleased, and wrapped her arm around Serena's long, slender waist. "Darling, I'd like you to meet my special friend, Cyrus Rose," she said. "Cyrus, this is Serena."

"Stunning," Cyrus Rose boomed. He kissed Serena on both cheeks, and hugged her a little too tightly. "She's a good hugger, too," Cyrus added, patting Serena on the hip.

Serena giggled, but she didn't flinch. She'd spent a lot of time in Europe in the past two years, and she was used to being hugged by harmless, horny European gropers who found her completely irresistible. She was a full-on groper magnet.

"Serena and Blair are best, best, *best* friends," Eleanor Waldorf explained to Cyrus. "But Serena went away to Hanover Academy in eleventh grade and spent this summer traveling. It was so hard for poor Blair with you gone this past year, Serena," Eleanor said, growing misty-eyed. "Especially with the divorce. But you're back now. Blair will be so *pleased.*"

"Where is she?" Serena asked eagerly, her perfect, pale skin glowing pink with the prospect of seeing her old friend again. She stood on tip-toe and craned her head to look for Blair, but she soon found herself surrounded by parents—the Archibalds, the Coateses, the Basses, and Mr. Farkas—who each took turns kissing her and welcoming her back.

Serena hugged them happily. These people were home to her, and she'd been gone a long time. She could hardly wait for life to return to the way it used to be. She and Blair would walk to school together, spend Double Photography in Sheep Meadow in Central Park, lying on their backs, taking pictures of pigeons and clouds, smoking and drinking Coke and feeling like hard-core artistes. They would have cocktails at the Star Lounge in the Tribeca Star Hotel again, which always turned into sleepover parties because they would get too drunk to get home, so they'd spend the night in the suite Chuck Bass's family kept there. They would sit on Blair's four-poster bed and watch Audrey Hepburn movies, wearing vintage lingerie and drinking gin and lime juice. They would cheat on their Latin tests like they always did—*amor, amas, amat* was still tattooed on the inside of Serena's elbow in permanent marker (thank God for three-quarter length sleeves!). They'd drive around Serena's parents' estate in Ridgefield, Connecticut, in the caretaker's old Buick station wagon, singing the stupid hymns they sang in school and acting like crazy old ladies. They'd pee in the downstairs entrances to their classmates' brownstones and then ring the doorbells and run away. They'd take Blair's little brother, Tyler, to the Lower East Side and leave him there to see how long it took for him to find his way home—a work of charity, really, since Tyler was now the most street-wise boy at St. George's. They'd go out dancing with a huge group and lose ten pounds just from sweating in their leather pants. As if they needed to lose the weight. They would go back to being their regular old fabulous selves, just like always. Serena couldn't wait.

"Got you a drink," Chuck Bass said, elbowing the clusters of parents out of the way and handing Serena a tumbler of whiskey. "Welcome back," he added, ducking down to kiss Serena's cheek and missing it intentionally, so that his lips landed on her mouth.

"You haven't changed," Serena said, accepting the drink. She took a long sip. "So, did you miss me?"

"Miss you? The question is, did you miss *me*?" Chuck said. "Come on, babe, spill. What are you doing back here? What happened? Do you have a boyfriend?"

"Oh, come on, Chuck," Serena said, squeezing his hand. "You know I came back because I want you so badly. I've always wanted you."

Chuck took a step back and cleared his throat, his face flushed. She'd caught him off guard, a rare feat.

"Well, I'm all booked up for this month, but I can put you on the waiting list," Chuck said huffily, trying to regain his composure.

But Serena was barely listening to him anymore. Her dark blue eyes scanned the room, looking for the two people she wanted to see most, Blair and Nate.

Finally Serena found them. Nate was standing by the doorway to the hall, and Blair was standing just behind him, her head bowed, fiddling with the buttons on her black cardigan. Nate was looking directly at Serena, and when her gaze met his, he bit his bottom lip the way he always did when he was embarrassed. And then he smiled.

That smile. Those eyes. That face.

"Come here," Serena mouthed at him, waving her hand.

Her heart sped up as Nate began walking toward her. He looked better than she remembered, *much* better.

Nate's heart was beating even faster than hers.

"Hey, you," Serena breathed when Nate hugged her. He smelled just like he always smelled. Like the cleanest, most delicious boy alive. Tears came to Serena's eyes and she pressed her face into Nate's chest. Now she was really home.

Nate's cheeks turned pink. *Calm down,* he told himself. But he couldn't calm down. He felt like picking her up and twirling her around and kissing her face over and over. *"I love you!"* he wanted to shout, but he didn't. He couldn't.

Nate was the only son of a navy captain and a French society hostess. His father was a master sailor and extremely handsome, but a little lacking in the hugs department. His mother was the complete opposite, always fawning over Nate and prone to emotional fits during which she would lock herself in her bedroom with a bottle of champagne and call her sister on her yacht in Monaco. Poor Nate was always on the verge of saying how he really felt, but he didn't want to make a scene or say something he might regret later. Instead, he kept quiet and let other people steer the boat, while he laid back and enjoyed the steady rocking of the waves.

He might look like a stud, but he was actually pretty weak.

"So, what have you been up to?" Nate asked Serena, trying to breathe normally. "We missed you."

Notice that he wasn't even brave enough to say, "*I* missed you"?

"What have I been up to?" Serena repeated. She giggled. "If you only knew, Nate. I've been so, so *bad*!"

Nate clenched his fists involuntarily. Man oh man, had he missed her.

★　　★　　★

Ignored as usual, Chuck slunk away from Serena and Nate and crossed the room to Blair, who was once again standing with Kati and Isabel.

"A thousand bucks says she got kicked out," Chuck told them. "And doesn't she look fucked? I think she's been *thoroughly* fucked. Maybe she had some sort of prostitution ring going on up there. The Merry Madam of Hanover Academy," he added, laughing at his own stupid joke.

"I think she looks kind of spaced out, too," Kati said. "Maybe she's on heroin."

"Or some prescription drug," Isabel said. "You know, like, Valium or Prozac. Maybe she's gone totally nuts."

"She could've been making her own E," Kati agreed. "She was always good at science."

"I heard she joined some kind of cult," Chuck offered. "Like, she's been brainwashed and now all she thinks about is sex and she like, has to do it all the time."

When is dinner going to be ready? Blair wondered, tuning out her friends' ridiculous speculations.

She had forgotten how pretty Serena's hair was. How perfect her skin was. How long and thin her legs were. What Nate's eyes looked like when he looked at her—like he never wanted to blink. He never looked at Blair that way.

"Hey Blair, Serena must have told you she was coming back," Chuck said. "Come on, tell us. What's the deal?"

Blair stared back at him blankly, her small, fox-like face turning red. The truth was, she hadn't really spoken to Serena in over a year.

At first, when Serena had gone to boarding school after sophomore year, Blair had really missed her. But it soon became apparent how much easier it was to shine without Serena around. Suddenly *Blair* was the prettiest, the smartest, the hippest, most happening girl in the room. She became the one everyone looked to. So Blair stopped missing Serena so much. She'd felt a little guilty for not staying in touch, but even that had worn off when she'd received Serena's flip and impersonal e-mails describing all the fun she was having at boarding school.

"Hitchhiked to Vermont to go snowboarding and spent the night dancing with the hottest guys!"

"Crazy night last night. Damn, my head hurts!"

The last news Blair had received was a postcard this past summer:

"Blair: Turned seventeen on Bastille Day. France rocks!! Miss you!!! Love, Serena," was all it said.

Blair had tucked the postcard into her old Fendi shoebox with all the other mementos from their friendship. A friendship she would cherish forever, but which she'd thought of as over until now.

Serena was back. The lid was off the shoebox, and everything would go back to the way it was before she left. As always, it would be Serena and Blair, Blair and Serena, with Blair playing the smaller, fatter, mousier, less witty best friend of the blond über-girl, Serena van der Woodsen.

Or not. Not if Blair could help it.

"You must be so excited Serena's here!" Isabel chirped. But when she saw the look on Blair's face, she changed her tune. "Of *course* Constance took her back. It's so typical. They're too desperate to lose any of us." Isabel lowered her voice. "I heard last spring Serena was fooling around with some townie up in New Hampshire. She had an abortion," she added.

"I bet it wasn't her first one either," Chuck said. "Just look at her."

And so they did. All four of them looked at Serena, who was still chatting happily with Nate. Chuck saw the girl he'd wanted to sleep with since he could remember wanting to sleep with girls—first grade, maybe? Kati saw the girl she'd been copying since she started shopping for her own clothes—third grade? Isabel saw the girl who'd gotten to be an angel with wings made out of real feathers at the Church of the Heavenly Rest Christmas pageant, while Isabel was a lowly shepherd and had to wear a burlap sack. Third grade again. Both Kati and Isabel saw the girl who would inevitably steal Blair away from them and leave them with only each other, which was too dull to even think about. And Blair saw Serena, her best friend, the girl she would always love and hate. The girl she could never measure up to and had tried so hard to replace. The girl she'd wanted everyone to forget.

For about ten seconds Blair thought about telling her friends the truth: She didn't *know* Serena was coming back. But how would that look? Blair was supposed to be plugged in, and how plugged in would she sound if she admitted she knew nothing about Serena's return, while her friends seemed to know so much? Blair couldn't very well stand there and say nothing. That would be too obvious. She *always* had something to say. Besides, who wanted to hear the truth when the truth was so incredibly boring? Blair lived for drama. Here was her chance.

Blair cleared her throat. "It all happened very . . . suddenly," she said mysteriously.

She looked down and fiddled with the little ruby ring on the middle finger of her right hand. The film was rolling, and Blair was getting warmed up.

"I think Serena is pretty messed up about it. But I promised her I wouldn't say anything," she added.

Her friends nodded as if they understood completely. It sounded serious and juicy, and best of all it sounded like Serena had confided everything to Blair. If only Blair could script the rest of the movie, she'd wind up with the boy for sure. And Serena could play the girl who falls off the cliff and cracks her skull on a rock and is eaten alive by hungry vultures, never to be seen again.

"Careful, Blair," Chuck warned, nodding at Serena and Nate, who were still talking in low voices over by the wet bar, their eyes never straying from each other's faces. "Looks like Serena's already found her next victim."

s & n

Serena was holding Nate's hand loosely in hers, swinging it back and forth.

"Remember Buck Naked?" she asked him, laughing softly.

Nate chuckled, still embarrassed, even after all these years. Buck Naked was Nate's alter ego, invented at a party in eighth grade, when most of them had gotten drunk for the first time. After drinking six beers, Nate had taken his shirt off, and Serena and Blair had drawn a goofy, buck-toothed face on his torso in black marker. For some reason the face brought out the devil in Nate, and he started a drinking game. Everyone sat in a circle and Nate stood in the middle, holding a Latin textbook and shouting out verbs for them to conjugate. The first person to mess up had to drink and kiss Buck Naked. Of course they all messed up, boys and girls alike, so Buck got a lot of action that night. The next morning, Nate tried to pretend it hadn't happened, but the proof was inked on his skin. It took weeks for Buck to wash off in the shower.

"And what about the Red Sea?" Serena said. She studied Nate's face. Neither of them was smiling now.

"The Red Sea," Nate repeated, drowning in the deep blue lakes of her eyes. Of course he remembered. How could he forget?

One hot August weekend, the summer after tenth grade,

Nate had been in the city with his dad, while the rest of the Archibald family was still in Maine. Serena was up in her country house in Ridgefield, Connecticut, so bored she'd painted each of her fingernails and toenails a different color. Blair was at the Waldorf castle in Gleneagles, Scotland, at her aunt's wedding. But that hadn't stopped her two best friends from having fun without her. When Nate called, Serena hopped right on the New Haven line into Grand Central Station.

Nate met Serena on the platform. She stepped off the train wearing a light blue silk slip dress and pink rubber flip-flops. Her yellow hair hung loose, just touching her bare shoulders. She wasn't carrying a bag, not even a wallet or keys. To Nate, she looked like an angel. How lucky he was. Life didn't get any better than the moment when Serena flip-flopped down the platform, threw her arms around his neck, and kissed him on the lips. That wonderful, surprising kiss.

First they had martinis at the little bar upstairs by the Vanderbilt Avenue entrance to Grand Central. Then they got a cab straight up Park Avenue to Nate's Eighty-second Street townhouse. His father was entertaining some foreign bankers and was going to be out until very late, so Serena and Nate had the place to themselves. Oddly enough, it was the first time they'd ever been alone together and *noticed*.

It didn't take long.

They sat out in the garden, drinking beer and smoking cigarettes. Nate was wearing a long-sleeved polo shirt, and the weather was extremely hot, so he took it off. His shoulders were scattered with tiny freckles, and his back was muscled and tan from hours at the docks, building a sailboat with his father up in Maine.

Serena was hot too, so she climbed into the fountain. She sat on the marble Venus de Milo statue's knee, splashing herself with water until her dress was soaked through.

It wasn't difficult to see who the real goddess was. Venus looked like a lumpy pile of marble compared to Serena. Nate staggered over to the fountain and got in with her, and soon they were tearing the rest of each other's clothes off. It was August after all. The only way to tolerate the city in August is to get naked.

Nate was worried about the security cameras trained on his parents' house at all times, front and back, so he led Serena inside and up to his parents' bedroom.

The rest is history.

They both had sex for the first time. It was awkward and painful and exciting and fun, and so sweet they forgot to be embarrassed. It was exactly the way you'd want your first time to be, and they had no regrets. Afterwards, they turned on the television, which was tuned to the History Channel, a documentary about the Red Sea. Serena and Nate lay in bed, holding each other and looking up at the clouds through the skylight overhead, while they listened to the narrator of the program talk about Moses parting the Red Sea.

Serena thought that was hilarious.

"You parted my Red Sea!" she howled, wrestling Nate against the pillows.

Nate laughed and rolled her up in the sheet like a mummy. "And now I will leave you here as a sacrifice to the Holy Land!" he said in a deep, horror-movie voice.

And he did leave her, for a little while. He got up and ordered a huge feast of Chinese food and bad white wine, and they lay in bed and ate and drank, and he parted her Red Sea once again before the sky grew dark and the stars twinkled in the skylight.

A week later, Serena went away to boarding school at Hanover Academy, while Nate and Blair stayed behind in New York. Ever since, Serena had spent every vacation away—the Austrian Alps at

Christmas, the Dominican Republic for Easter, the summer traveling in Europe. This was the first time she'd been back, the first time
she and Nate had seen each other since the parting of the Red Sea.

"Blair doesn't know, does she?" Serena asked Nate quietly.

Blair who? Nate thought, with a momentary case of amnesia.
He shook his head. "No," he said. "If you haven't told her, she
doesn't know."

But Chuck Bass knew, which was almost worse. Nate had
blurted the information out at a party only two nights ago in a
drunken fit of complete stupidity. They'd been doing shots, and
Chuck had asked, "So, Nate. What was your all time best fuck?
That is, if you've done it all yet."

"Well, I did it with Serena van der Woodsen," Nate had
bragged, like an idiot.

And Chuck wasn't going to keep it a secret for long. It was
way too juicy and way too useful. Chuck didn't need to read that
book *How to Win Friends and Influence People*. He fucking wrote
it. Although he wasn't doing so well in the friends department.

Serena didn't seem to notice Nate's uncomfortable silence.
She sighed, bowing her head to rest it on his shoulder. She no
longer smelled like Chanel's *Cristalle* like she always used to. She
smelled like honey and sandalwood and lilies—her own essential-oil mixture. It was very Serena, utterly irresistible, but if anyone else tried to wear it, it would probably smell like dog poo.

"Shit. I missed you like crazy, Nate," she said. "I wish you
could've seen the stuff I pulled. I was so bad."

"What do you mean? What did you do that was so bad?"
Nate asked, with a mixture of dread and anticipation. For a
brief second he imagined her hosting orgies in her dorm room
at Hanover Academy and having affairs with older men in hotel
rooms in Paris. He wished he could've visited her in Europe this
summer. He'd always wanted to do it in a hotel.

"And I've been such a horrible friend, too," Serena went on. "I've barely even talked to Blair since I left. And so much has happened. I can already tell she's mad. She hasn't even said hello."

"She's not mad," Nate said. "Maybe she's just feeling shy."

Serena flashed him a look. "Right," she said mockingly. "Blair's feeling shy. Since when has Blair ever been shy?"

"Well, she's not mad," Nate insisted.

Serena shrugged. "Well, anyway, I'm so psyched to be back here with you guys. We'll do all the things we used to do. Blair and I will cut class and meet you on the roof of the Met, and then we'll run down to that old movie theater by the Plaza Hotel and see some weirdo film until cocktail hour starts. And you and Blair will stay together forever and I'll be the maid of honor at your wedding. And we'll be happy ever after, just like in the movies."

Nate frowned.

"Don't make that face, Nate," Serena said, laughing. "That doesn't sound so bad, does it?"

Nate shrugged. "No, I guess it sounds okay," he said, although he clearly didn't believe it.

"What sounds okay?" a surly voice demanded.

Startled, Nate and Serena tore their eyes away from each other. It was Chuck, and with him were Kati, Isabel, and, last but not least, Blair, looking very shy indeed.

Chuck clapped Nate on the back. "Sorry, Nate," he said. "But you can't bogey the van der Woodsen all night, you know."

Nate snorted and tipped back his glass. Only ice was left.

Serena looked at Blair. Or at least, she tried to. Blair was making a big deal of pulling up her black stockings, working them inch by inch from her bony ankles up to her bony knees, and up around her tennis-muscled thighs. So Serena gave up and kissed first Kati, then Isabel, and then she made her way to Blair.

There was only a limited amount of time Blair could spend pulling up her tights before it got ridiculous. When Serena was only inches away from her, she looked up and pretended to be surprised.

"Hey Blair," Serena said excitedly. She put her hands on the shorter girl's shoulders and bent down to kiss both of her cheeks. "I'm so sorry I didn't call you before I came back. I wanted to. But things have been *so* crazy. I have so much to tell you!"

Chuck, Kati, and Isabel all nudged each other and stared at Blair. It was pretty obvious she had lied. She didn't know anything about Serena coming back.

Blair's face heated up.

Busted.

Nate noticed the tension, but he thought it was for an entirely different reason. Had Chuck told Blair already? Was *he* busted? Nate couldn't tell. Blair wasn't even looking at him.

It was a chilly moment. Not the kind of moment you'd expect to have with your oldest, closest friends.

Serena's eyes darted from one face to another. Clearly she had said something wrong, and she quickly guessed what it was. *I'm such an asshole*, she scolded herself.

"I mean, I'm sorry I didn't call you *last night*. I literally just got back from Ridgefield. My parents have been hiding me there until they figured out what to do with me. I have been *so bored*."

Nice save.

She waited for Blair to smile gratefully for covering for her, but all Blair did was glance at Kati and Isabel to see if they'd noticed the slip. Blair was acting strange, and Serena fought down a rising panic. Maybe Nate was wrong, maybe Blair really was mad at her. Serena had missed out on so much. The divorce, for instance. Poor Blair.

"It must really stink without your dad around," Serena said.

"But your mom looks so good, and Cyrus is kind of sweet, once you get used to him." She giggled.

But Blair still wasn't smiling. "Maybe," she said, staring out the window at the hot-dog stand. "I guess I'm still not used to him."

All six of them were silent for a long, tense moment.

What they needed was one more good, stiff drink.

Nate rattled the ice cubes in his glass. "Who wants another?" he offered. "I'll make them."

Serena held out her glass. "Thanks, Nate," she said. "I'm so fucking thirsty. They locked the damned booze cabinet up in Ridgefield. Can you believe it?"

Blair shook her head. "No, thanks," she said.

"If I have another, I'll be hungover at school tomorrow," Kati said.

Isabel laughed. "You're always hungover at school," she said. She handed Nate her glass. "Here, I'll split mine with Kati."

"Let me give you a hand," Chuck offered. But before he could get very far, Mrs. van der Woodsen joined them, touching her daughter's arm.

"Serena," her mother said. "Eleanor would like us all to sit down. She made an extra place next to Blair for you, so you two girls can catch up."

Serena cast an anxious glance at Blair, but Blair had already turned away and was headed for the table, sitting down next to her eleven-year-old brother, Tyler, who had been at his place for over an hour, reading *Rolling Stone* magazine. Tyler's idol was that movie director, Cameron Crowe, who had toured with Led Zeppelin when he was only fifteen. Tyler refused to listen to CDs, insisting that real vinyl records were the only way to go. Blair worried her brother was turning into a loser.

Serena steeled herself and pulled up a chair in the space next to Blair.

"Blair, I'm sorry I've been such a complete asshole," she said, removing her linen napkin from its silver ring and spreading it out on her lap. "Your parents splitting up must have totally sucked."

Blair shrugged and grabbed a fresh sourdough roll from a basket on the table. She tore the roll in half and stuffed one half into her mouth. The other guests were still making their way toward the table and figuring out where to sit. Blair knew it was rude to eat before everyone was seated, but if her mouth was full, she couldn't talk, and she really didn't feel like talking.

"I wish I'd been here," Serena said, watching Blair smear the other half of her roll with a thick slab of French butter. "But I had a crazy year. I have the most insane stories to tell you."

Blair nodded and chewed her roll slowly, like a cow chewing its cud. Serena waited for Blair to ask her what kind of stories, but Blair didn't say anything, she just kept on chewing. She didn't want to hear about all the fabulous things Serena had done while she was away and Blair had been stuck at home, watching her parents fight over antique chairs that nobody sat on, teacups nobody used, and ugly, expensive paintings.

Serena had wanted to tell Blair about Charles, the only Rastafarian at Hanover Academy, who'd asked her to elope with him to Jamaica. About Nicholas, the French college guy who never wore underwear and who'd chased her train in a tiny Fiat all the way from Paris to Milan. About smoking hash in Amsterdam and sleeping in a park with a group of drunk prostitutes because she forgot where she was staying. She wanted to tell Blair how much it sucked to find out that Hanover Academy wouldn't take her back senior year simply because she'd blown off the first few weeks of school. She wanted to tell Blair how scared she was to go back to Constance tomorrow because she hadn't exactly been studying very hard in the last year and she felt so completely out of touch.

But Blair wasn't interested. She grabbed another roll and took a big bite.

"Wine, miss?" Esther said, standing at Serena's left with the bottle.

"Yes, thank you," Serena said. She watched the Côte du Rhone spill into her glass and thought of the Red Sea once more. *Maybe Blair does know*, she thought. Was that what this was all about? Was that why she was acting so weird?

Serena glanced at Nate, four chairs down on the right, but he was deep in conversation with her father. Talking about boats no doubt.

"So, you and Nate are still totally together?" Serena said, taking a risk. "I bet you guys wind up married."

Blair gulped her wine, her little ruby ring rattling against the glass. She reached for the butter, slapping a great big wad on her roll.

"Hello? Blair?" Serena said, nudging her friend's arm. "Are you okay?"

"Yeah," Blair slurred. It was less an answer to Serena's question than a vague, general statement made to fill a blank space while she was tending to her roll. "I'm fine."

Esther brought out the duck and the acorn squash soufflé and the wilted chard and the lingonberry sauce, and the table was filled with the sound of clanking plates and silver and murmurs of "delicious." Blair heaped her plate high with food and attacked it as if she hadn't eaten in weeks. She didn't care if she made herself sick, as long as she didn't have to talk to Serena.

"Whoa," Serena said, watching Blair stuff her face. "You must be hungry."

Blair nodded and shoveled a forkful of chard into her mouth. She washed it down with a gulp of wine. "I'm starving," she said.

"So, Serena," Cyrus Rose called down from the head of the table. "Tell me about France. Your mother says you were in the South of France this summer. Is it true the French girls don't wear tops on the beach?"

"Yes, it's true," Serena said. She raised one eyebrow playfully. "But it's not just the French girls. I never wore a top down there, either. How else could I get a decent tan?"

Blair gagged on an enormous bite of soufflé and spat it into her wine. It floated on the surface of the crimson liquid like a soggy dumpling until Esther whisked it away and brought her a clean glass.

No one noticed. Serena had the table's attention, and she kept her audience captive with stories of her travels in Europe right through dessert. When Blair had finished her second plate of duck, she ate a huge bowl full of chocolate-laced tapioca pudding, tuning out Serena's voice as she spooned it into her mouth. Finally her stomach rebelled, and she shot up suddenly, scraping her chair back and running down the hall to her bedroom, straight into its adjoining bathroom.

"Blair?" Serena called after her. She stood up. "Excuse me," she said, and hurried away to see what was the matter. She didn't have to move that fast; Blair wasn't going anywhere.

When Chuck saw Blair get up from the table, and then Serena, he nodded knowingly and nudged Isabel with his elbow. "Blair's getting the dirt," he whispered. "Fucking awesome."

Nate watched the two girls flee the table with a mounting sense of unease. He was pretty sure the only thing girls talked about in the bathroom was sex.

And mostly, he'd be right.

Blair kneeled over the toilet and stuck her middle finger as far down her throat as it would go. Her eyes began to tear and then her stomach convulsed. She'd done this before, many times. It was disgusting and horrible, and she knew she shouldn't do it, but at least she'd feel better when it was over.

The door to her bathroom was only half closed, and Serena could hear her friend retching inside.

"Blair, it's me," Serena said quietly. "Are you okay?"

"I'll be out in a minute," Blair snapped, wiping her mouth. She stood up and flushed the toilet.

Serena pushed the door open and Blair turned and glared at her. "I'm fine," Blair said. "Really."

Serena put the lid down on the toilet seat and sat down. "Oh, don't be such a bitch, Blair," she said, exasperated. "What's the deal? It's me, remember? We know everything about each other."

Blair reached for her toothbrush and toothpaste. "We used to," she said and began brushing her teeth furiously. She spat out a wad of green foam. "When was the last time we talked, anyway? Like, the summer before last?"

Serena looked down at her scuffed brown leather boots. "I know. I'm sorry. I suck," she said.

Blair rinsed her toothbrush off and stuck it back in the holder. She stared at her reflection in the bathroom mirror. "Well, you missed a lot," she said, wiping a smudge of mascara from beneath her eye with the tip of her pinky. "I mean, last year was really . . . different." She'd been about to say "hard," but "hard" made her sound like a victim. Like she'd barely survived without Serena around. "Different" was better.

Blair glanced down at Serena sitting on the toilet, with a sudden sense of power. "Nate and I have become really close, you know. We tell each other everything."

Yeah, right.

The two girls eyed each other warily for a moment. Then Serena shrugged. "Well don't worry about me and Nate," she said. "We're just friends, you know that. And besides, I'm tired of boys."

The corners of Blair's mouth curled up. Serena obviously wanted her to ask why, *why* was she tired of boys? But Blair wasn't going to give her the satisfaction. She tugged her sweater down and glanced at her reflection one more time. "I'll see you back in there," she said, and abruptly left the bathroom.

Shit, Serena thought, but she stayed where she was. It was no use going after Blair now, while she was obviously in such a crappy mood. Things would be better tomorrow at school. She and Blair would have one of their famous heart-to-hearts in the lunchroom over lemon yogurts and romaine lettuce. It wasn't like they could just stop being friends.

Serena stood up and examined her eyebrows in the bathroom mirror, using Blair's tweezers to pluck a few stray hairs. She pulled a tube of Urban Decay *Gash* lip gloss from her pocket and smeared another layer on her lips. Then she picked up Blair's hairbrush and began brushing her hair. Finally, she peed and rejoined the dinner party, forgetting her lip gloss on Blair's sink.

When Serena sat down, Blair was eating her second helping of pudding, and Nate was drawing a small-scale picture of his kick-ass sailboat for Cyrus on the back of a matchbook. Across the table Chuck raised his wine glass to clink it with Serena's. She had no idea what she was toasting, but she was always up for anything.

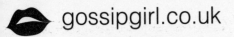
Disclaimer: All the real names of places, people, and events have been altered or abbreviated to protect the innocent. Namely, me.

hey people!

S SEEN DEALING ON STEPS OF MET

Well, we're certainly off to a good start. You sent me tons of e-mail, and I had the best time reading it all. Thanks so much. Doesn't it feel good to be bad?

Your E-Mail

Q:
hey gossip girl,
i heard about a girl up in New Hampshire who the police found naked a field, with a bunch of dead chickens. ew. they thought she was into some kind of voodoo shit or something. do you think that was *S*? i mean it sounds like her, right? l8ter.
—catee3

A:
Dear Catee3,
I don't know, but I wouldn't be surprised. *S* is a big fan of chickens. Once, in the park, I saw her eat a whole bucket of fried chicken without stopping for air. But supposedly she'd been hitting the bong pretty heavily that day.
—GG

Q:
Dear GG,
My name starts with *S* and I have blond hair!!! I also just came back from boarding school to my old school in NYC. I was just so sick of all the rules, like no drinking or smoking or boys in your room. : (Anyway, I have my own apartment now and I'm having a party next Saturday—wanna come? :-)
—S969

A: Dear S969,
The *S* I'm writing about still lives with her parents like most of us seventeen-year-olds, you lucky bitch.
—GG

Q: whatsup, gossip girl?
last night some guys I know got a handfull of pills from some blond chick on the steps of the metropolitan museum of art. they had the letter *S* stamped all over them. coincidence, or what?
—N00name

A: Dear N00name,
Whoa, is all I have to say.
—GG

3 GUYS AND 2 GIRLS

I and *K* are going to have a little trouble fitting into those cute dresses they picked up at Bendel's if they keep stopping in at the **3 Guys Coffee Shop** for hot chocolate and French fries every day. I went in there myself to see what the fuss was about, and I guess I could say my waiter was cute, if you like ear fuzz, but the food is worse than at **Jackson Hole** and the average person in there is like, 100 years old.

Sightings

C was seen in **Tiffany**, picking up another pair of monogrammed cuf-flinks for a party. Hello? I'm waiting for my invite. *B*'s mother was seen holding hands with her new man in **Cartier**. Hmmm, when's the wed-ding? Also seen: a girl bearing a striking resemblance to *S,* coming out of an STD clinic on the Lower East Side. She was wearing a thick black wig and big sunglasses. Some disguise. And very late last night, *S* was seen leaning out her bedroom window over Fifth Avenue, looking a little lost.

Well, don't jump, sweetie, things are just starting to get good.

That's all for now. See you in school tomorrow.

You know you love me,

gossip girl

hark the herald angels sing

"Welcome back, girls," Mrs. McLean said, standing behind the podium at the front of the school auditorium. "I hope you all had a terrific long weekend. I spent the weekend in Vermont, and it was absolutely heavenly."

All seven hundred students at the Constance Billard School for Girls, kindergarten through twelfth grade, and its fifty faculty and staff members tittered discreetly. Everyone knew Mrs. McLean had a girlfriend up in Vermont. Her name was Vonda, and she drove a tractor. Mrs. McLean had a tattoo on her inner thigh that said, "Ride Me, Vonda."

It's true, swear to God.

Mrs. McLean, or Mrs. M, as the girls called her, was their headmistress. It was her job to put forth the cream of the crop— send the girls off to the best colleges, the best marriages, the best lives—and she was very good at what she did. She had no patience for losers, and if she caught one of her girls acting like a loser—persistently calling in sick or doing poorly on the SATs—she would call in the shrinks, counselors, and tutors and make sure the girl got the personal attention she needed to get good grades, high scores, and a warm welcome to the college of her choice.

Mrs. M also didn't tolerate meanness. Constance was supposed to be a school free of cliques and prejudice of any sort. Her favorite saying was, "When you *ass*ume, you make an *ass* out of *u* and *me*." The slightest slander of one girl by another was punished with a day in isolation and a seriously difficult essay assignment. But those punishments were a rare necessity. Mrs. M was blissfully ignorant of what really went on in the school. She certainly couldn't hear the whispering going on in the very back of the auditorium, where the seniors sat.

"I thought you said Serena was coming back today," Rain Hoffstetter whispered to Isabel Coates.

That morning, Blair and Kati and Isabel and Rain had all met on their usual stoop around the corner for cigarettes and coffee before school started. They had been doing the same thing every morning for two years, and they half expected Serena to join them. But school had started ten minutes ago, and Serena still hadn't shown up.

Blair couldn't help feeling annoyed at Serena for creating even more mystery around her return than there already was. Her friends were practically squirming in their seats, eager to catch their first glimpse of Serena, as if she were some kind of celebrity.

"She's probably too drugged up to come to school today," Isabel whispered back. "I swear, she spent like, an hour in the bathroom last night at Blair's house. Who knows what she was doing in there."

"I heard she's selling these pills with the letter S stamped on them. She's completely addicted to them," Kati told Rain.

"Wait till you see her," Isabel said. "She's a total mess."

"Yeah," Rain whispered back. "I heard she'd started some kind of voodoo cult up in New Hampshire."

Kati giggled. "I wonder if she'll ask us to join."

"Hello?" said Isabel. "She can dance around naked with chickens all she wants, but I don't want to be there. No way."

"Where can you get live chickens in the city, anyway?" Kati asked.

"Gross," Rain said.

"Now, I'd like to begin by singing a hymn. If you would please rise and open up your hymnals to page forty-three," Mrs. M instructed.

Mrs. Weeds, the frizzy-haired hippie music teacher, began banging out the first few chords of the familiar hymn on the piano in the corner; then all seven hundred girls stood up and began to sing.

Their voices floated down Ninety-third Street, where Serena van der Woodsen was just turning the corner, cursing herself for being late. She hadn't woken up this early since her eleventh-grade final exams at Hanover last June, and she'd forgotten how badly it sucked.

> *"Hark the herald angels si-ing!*
> *Glo-ry to the newborn king!*
> *Peace on Earth and mercy mi-ild,*
> *God and sin-ners reconciled."*

Constance ninth grader Jenny Humphrey silently mouthed the words, sharing with her neighbor the hymnal which Jenny herself had been commissioned to pen in her exceptional calligraphy. It had taken all summer, and the hymnals were beautiful. In three years the Pratt Institute of Art and Design would be knocking her door down. Still, Jenny felt sick with embarrassment every time they used the hymnals, which was why she couldn't sing out loud. To sing aloud seemed like an act of bravado, as if she were saying, "Look at me, I'm singing along to the hymnals *I* made! Aren't I cool?"

Jenny preferred to be invisible. She was a curly-haired, tiny little freshman, so invisible wasn't a hard thing to be. Actually, it would have been easier if her boobs weren't so incredibly huge. At fourteen, she was a 34D.

Can you imagine?

"Hark the heavenly host proclaims,
Christ i-is born in Beth-le-hem!"

Jenny was standing at the end of a row of folding chairs, next to the big auditorium windows overlooking Ninety-third Street. Suddenly a movement out on the street caught her eye. Blond hair flying. Burberry plaid coat. Scuffed brown suede boots. New maroon uniform—odd choice, but she made it work. It looked like . . . it couldn't be . . . could it possibly . . . No! . . . Was it?

Yes, *it was.*

A moment later Serena van der Woodsen pushed open the heavy wooden door of the auditorium and stood in front of it, looking for her class. She was out of breath and her hair was windblown. Her cheeks were rosy and her eyes were bright from running the twelve blocks up Fifth Avenue to school. She looked even more perfect than Jenny had remembered.

"Oh. My. God," Rain whispered to Kati in the back of the room. "Did she like, pick up her clothes at a homeless shelter on the way here?"

"She didn't even brush her hair," Isabel giggled. "I wonder where she slept last night."

Mrs. Weeds ended the hymn with a crashing chord.

Mrs. M cleared her throat. "And now, a moment of silence for those less fortunate than we are. Especially for the Native Americans that were slaughtered in the founding of this country, of whom we ask no hard feelings for celebrating Columbus Day yesterday," she said.

The room fell silent. Well, almost.

"Look, see how Serena's resting her hands on her stomach? She's probably pregnant," Isabel Coates whispered to Rain Hoffstetter. "You only do that when you're pregnant."

"She could have had an abortion this morning. Maybe that's why she's late," Rain whispered back.

"My father gives money to Phoenix House," Kati told Laura Salmon. "I'm going to find out if Serena's been there. I bet that's why she came back halfway through term. She's been in rehab."

"I hear they're doing this thing in boarding school where they mix Comet and cinnamon and instant coffee and snort it. It's like speed, but it makes your skin turn green if you do it too long," Nicki Button piped up. "You go blind, and then you die."

Blair caught snippets of her friends' chatter, and it made her smile.

Mrs. M turned to nod at Serena.

"Girls, I'd like you all to welcome back our old friend Serena van der Woodsen. Serena will be rejoining the senior class today." Mrs. M smiled. "Why don't you find a seat, Serena?"

Serena walked lightly down the center aisle of the auditorium and sat down in an empty chair next to a chronic nose-picking second grader named Lisa Sykes.

Jenny could hardly contain herself. Serena van der Woodsen! She was *there*, in the same room, only a few feet away. So *real*. And so mature-looking now.

I wonder how many times she's done it, Jenny wondered to herself.

She imagined Serena and a blond Hanover boy leaning against the trunk of a big old tree, his coat wrapped around both of them. Serena had had to sneak out of her dorm without a coat. She was very cold, and she got tree sap in her hair, but it was worth it. Then Jenny pictured Serena and another imaginary boy on a ski lift. The ski lift got stuck and Serena climbed into the boy's lap to get warm. They began to kiss and they couldn't stop themselves. By the time they were done, the ski lift had started again and their skis were all tangled up, so they stayed on the chair and rode it downhill and did it again.

How cool, Jenny thought. Hands down, Serena van der Woodsen was absolutely the coolest girl in the entire world. Definitely cooler than any of the other seniors. And how cool to come in late, in the middle of the term, looking like *that*.

No matter how rich and fabulous you are, boarding school does have a way of making you look like a homeless person. A glamorous one, in Serena's case.

She hadn't had a haircut in over a year. Last night she'd worn it pulled back, but today it was down and looking pretty shaggy. Her boy's white oxford shirt was frayed in the collar and cuffs, and through it, her purple lace bra was visible. On her feet was her favorite pair of brown lace-up boots, and her black stockings had a big hole behind one knee. Worst of all, she'd had to buy all new uniforms, since she'd thrown hers down the garbage chute when she'd gone away to boarding school. Her new uniform was what stuck out the most.

The new uniforms were the plague of the sixth grade, which was the year Constance girls graduated from a tunic to a skirt. The new skirts were made out of polyester and had pleats that were unnaturally rigid. The material had a terrible, tacky sheen and came in a new color: maroon. It was hideous. And it was this maroon uniform that Serena had chosen to wear on her first day back at Constance. Plus, hers came all the way down to her knees! All of the other seniors were wearing the same old navy blue wool skirts they'd been wearing since sixth grade.

They'd grown so much their skirts were extremely short. The shorter the skirt, the cooler the girl.

Blair actually hadn't grown that much, so she'd secretly had hers shortened.

"What the fuck is she wearing, anyway?" Kati Farkas hissed.

"Maybe she thinks the maroon looks like Prada or something," Laura sniggered back.

"I think she's trying to make some kind of statement," Isabel whispered. "Like, look at me, I'm Serena, I'm beautiful, I can wear whatever I want."

And she can, Blair thought. That was one of the things that always infuriated her about Serena. She looked good in anything.

But never mind how Serena looked. What Jenny and every other person in the room wanted to know was: *Why is she back?*

They craned their necks to see. Did she have a black eye? Was she pregnant? Did she look stoned? Did she have all her teeth? Was there anything different about her at all?

"Is that a scar on her cheek?" Rain whispered.

"She was knifed one night dealing drugs," Kati whispered back. "I heard she had plastic surgery in Europe this summer, but they didn't do a very good job."

Mrs. McLean was reading out loud now. Serena sat back in her chair, crossed her legs, and closed her eyes, basking in the old familiar feeling of sitting in this room full of girls, listening to Mrs. M.'s voice. She didn't know why she'd been so nervous that morning before school. She'd overslept and gotten dressed in five minutes, ripping a hole in her black stocking with a jagged toenail. She'd chosen her brother Erik's frayed old shirt because it smelled like him. Erik had gone to the same boarding school as Serena, but now he was away at college, and she missed him terribly.

Just as she was leaving the apartment, her mother caught sight of her and would have made her change her clothes if Serena hadn't been so late.

"This weekend," her mother said, "we're going shopping, and I'm taking you to my salon. You can't go around looking like that here, Serena. I don't care how they let you dress in boarding school." Then she kissed her daughter on the cheek and went back to bed.

"Oh my God, I think she's asleep," Kati whispered to Laura.

"Maybe she's just tired," Laura whispered back. "I heard she got kicked out for sleeping with every boy on campus. There were notches in the wall above her bed. Her roommate told on her, that's the only way they found out."

"Plus, all those late-night chicken dances," Isabel added, sending the girls into a giggling frenzy.

Blair bit her lip, fighting back the laughter. It was just too funny.

s's other fan

If Jenny Humphrey could have heard what the girls in the senior class were saying about Serena van der Woodsen, her idol, she would have punched their lights out. The minute Prayers was dismissed, Jenny pushed past her classmates and darted out into the hallway to make a phone call. Her brother Daniel was going to totally lose his shit when she told him.

"Hello?" Daniel Humphrey answered his cell phone on the third ring. He was standing on the corner of Seventy-seventh Street and West End Avenue, outside Riverside Prep, smoking a cigarette. He squinted his dark brown eyes, trying to block out the harsh October sunlight. Dan wasn't into sun. He spent most of his free time in his room, reading morbid, existential-ist poetry about the bitter fate of being human. He was pale, his hair was shaggy, and he was rock-star thin.

Existentialism has a way of killing your appetite.

"Guess who's back?" Dan heard his little sister squeal excitedly into the phone.

Like Dan, Jenny was a bit of a loner, and when she needed someone to talk to, she always called him. She was the one who had bought them both cell phones.

"Jenny, can't this wait—" Dan started to say, sounding annoyed in the way that only older brothers can.

"Serena van der Woodsen!" Jenny interrupted him. "Serena is back at Constance. I saw her in Prayers. Can you believe it?"

Dan watched a plastic coffee-cup lid skitter down the sidewalk. A red Saab sped down West End Avenue through a yellow light. His socks felt damp inside his brown suede Hush Puppies. *Serena van der Woodsen.* He took a long drag on his Camel. His hands were shaking so much he almost missed his mouth.

"Dan?" his sister squeaked into the phone. "Can you hear me? Did you hear what I said? Serena is back. Serena van der Woodsen."

Dan sucked in his breath sharply. "Yeah, I heard you," he said, feigning disinterest. "So what?"

"So what?" Jenny said incredulously. "Oh, right, like you didn't just have a mini heart attack. You're so full of it, Dan."

"No, I'm serious," Dan said, pissily. "What are you calling me for? What do I care?"

Jenny sighed loudly. Dan could be so irritating. Why couldn't he just act happy for once? She was so tired of his pale, miserable, introspective-poet act.

"All right," she said. "Forget it. I'll talk to you later."

She clicked off and Dan shoved his cell phone back into the pocket of his faded black corduroys. He snatched a pack of cigarettes out of his back pocket and lit another one with the burning stub of the one he was already smoking. His thumbnail got singed, but he didn't even feel it.

Serena van der Woodsen.

They had first met at a party. No, that wasn't *exactly* true. Dan had *seen* her at a party, his party, the only one he'd ever had at his family's apartment on Ninety-ninth and West End Avenue.

It was April of eighth grade. The party was Jenny's idea, and their father, Rufus Humphrey, the infamous retired editor of lesser-known beat poets and a party animal himself, was happy to oblige. Their mother had already moved to Prague a few years before to "focus on her art." Dan invited his entire class and told them to invite as many people as they wanted. More than a hundred kids showed up, and Rufus kept the beer flowing out of a keg in the bathtub, getting many of the kids drunk for the first time. It was the best party Dan had ever been to, even if he did say so himself. Not because of the booze, but because Serena van der Woodsen was there. Never mind that she had gotten wasted and wound up playing a stupid Latin drinking game and kissing some guy's stomach with pictures scrawled all over it in magic marker. Dan couldn't keep his eyes off her.

Afterwards, Jenny told him that Serena went to her school, Constance, and from then on Jenny was his little emissary, reporting everything she'd seen Serena do, say, wear, etc., and informing Dan about any upcoming events where he might catch a glimpse of her again. Those events were rare. Not because there weren't a lot of them—there were—but because there weren't many Dan had even a chance of going to. Dan didn't inhabit the same world as Serena and Blair and Nate and Chuck. He wasn't anybody. He was just a regular kid.

For two years Dan followed Serena, yearningly, from a distance. He never spoke to her. When she went away to boarding school, he tried to forget about her, sure that he would never see her again, unless by some act of magic they wound up at the same college.

And now she was back.

Dan walked halfway down the block, then turned around and walked back again. His mind was racing. He could have another party. He could make invitations and get Jenny to slip one into Serena's locker at school. When Serena came to his apartment, Dan would walk right up to her and take her coat, and welcome her back to New York.

It rained every day you were gone, he'd say, poetically.

Then they would sneak into his father's library and take each other's clothes off and kiss on the leather couch in front of the fire. And when everyone left the party, they would share a bowl of Breyers coffee ice cream, Dan's favorite. From then on they would spend every minute together. They would even transfer to a coed high school like Trinity for the rest of senior year because they couldn't stand to be apart. Then they would go to Columbia and live in a studio apartment nearby with nothing in it but a huge bed. Serena's friends would try to lure her back to her old life, but no charity ball, no exclusive black-tie dinner, no expensive party favor could tempt her. She wouldn't care if she had to give up her trust fund and her great-grandmother's diamonds. Serena would be willing to live in squalor if it meant she could be with Dan.

"Fucking hell, we've only got five minutes until the bell rings," Dan heard someone say in an obnoxious voice.

Dan turned around, and sure enough, it was Chuck Bass, or "Scarf Boy," as Dan liked to call him, since Chuck was always wearing that ridiculous monogrammed cashmere scarf. Chuck was standing only twenty feet away with two of his senior Riverside Prep pals, Roger Paine and Jeffrey Prescott. They didn't speak to Dan or even nod to acknowledge his presence. Why should they? These boys took the Seventy-ninth Street crosstown bus through Central Park each morning to school from the swanky Upper East Side, only venturing to the West Side for school or to attend the odd party. They were in Dan's class at Riverside Prep, but they were certainly not in his *class*. He was nothing to them. They didn't even notice him.

"Dude," Chuck said to his friends. He lit a cigarette. Chuck smoked his cigarettes like they were joints, holding them between his index finger and thumb and sucking hard on the inhale.

Too pathetic for words.

"Guess who I saw last night?" Chuck said, blowing out a stream of gray smoke.

"Liv Tyler?" Jeffrey said.

"Yeah, and she was all over you, right?" Roger laughed.

"No, not her. Serena van der Woodsen," Chuck said.

Dan's ears perked up. He was about to head inside for class, but he lit another cigarette and stayed put so he could listen.

"Blair Waldorf's mom had this little party, and Serena was there with her parents," Chuck continued. "And she *was* all over me. She's, like, the sluttiest girl I've ever met." Chuck took another toke on his smoke.

"Really?" Jeffrey said.

"Yes, really. First of all, I just found out that she's been fucking Nate Archibald since tenth grade. And she's definitely gotten an education at boarding school, if you know what I mean. They had to get rid of her, she's so slutty."

"No way," Roger said. "Come on, dude, you don't get kicked out for being a slut."

"You do if you keep a record of every boy you slept with and get them hooked on the same drugs you're doing. Her parents had to go up there and get her. She was, like, taking over the school!" Chuck was getting really worked up. His face was turning red and he was spitting as he talked.

"I heard she's got diseases, too," he added. "Like, STDs. Someone saw her going into a clinic in the East Village. She was wearing a wig."

Chuck's friends shook their heads, grunting in amazement.

Dan had never heard such crap. Serena was no slut; she was perfect, wasn't she? *Wasn't she?*

That's yet to be determined.

"So, you guys hear about that bird party?" Roger asked. "You going?"

"What bird party?" Jeffrey said.

"That thing for the Central Park peregrine falcons?" Chuck said. "Yeah, Blair was telling me about it. It's in the old Barneys store." He took another drag on his cigarette. "Dude, every-body's going."

Everybody didn't include Dan, of course. But it very definite-ly included Serena van der Woodsen.

"They're sending out the invitations this week," Roger said. "It has a funny name, I can't remember what it is, something girly."

"*Kiss on the Lips*," Chuck said, stubbing out his cigarette with his obnoxious Church's of England shoes. "It's the *Kiss on the Lips* party."

"Oh, yeah," Jeffrey said. "And I bet there's going to be a lot more than kissing going on." He sniggered. "Especially if Serena's there."

The boys laughed, congratulating each other on their incred-ible wit.

Dan had had enough. He tossed his cigarette on the sidewalk only inches from Chuck's shoes and headed for the school doors. As he passed the three boys he turned his head and puckered his lips, making a smooching sound three times as if he were giving each boy a big fat kiss on the lips. Then he turned and went inside, banging the door shut behind him.

Kiss that, assholes.

at the heart of every fashion disaster is a hopeless romantic

"What I'm going for is tension," Vanessa Abrams explained to Constance's small Advanced Film Studies class. She was standing at the front of the room, presenting her idea for the film she was making. "I'm going to shoot the two of them talking on a park bench at night. Except you can't really hear what they're saying." Vanessa paused dramatically, waiting for one of her classmates to say something. Mr. Beckham, their teacher, was always telling them to keep their scenes alive with dialogue and action, and Vanessa was deliberately doing just the opposite.

"So there's no dialogue?" Mr. Beckham said from where he was standing in the back of the classroom. He was painfully aware that no one else in the class was listening to a word Vanessa was saying.

"You're going to hear the silence of the buildings and the bench and the sidewalk, and see the streetlights on their bodies. Then you'll see their hands move and their eyes talking. *Then* you'll hear them speak, but not much. It's a mood piece," Vanessa explained.

She reached for the slide projector's remote control and began clicking through slides of the black-and-white pictures she'd taken to demonstrate the look she was going for in her short film. A wooden park bench. A slab of pavement. A manhole cover. A pigeon pecking at a used condom. A wad of gum perched on the edge of a garbage can.

"Ha!" someone exclaimed from the back of the room. It was Blair Waldorf, laughing out loud as she read the note Rain Hoffstetter had just passed her.

> *For a good time*
> *call Serena v.d. Woodsen*
> *Get it — VD??*

Vanessa glared at Blair. Film was Vanessa's favorite class, the only reason she came to school at all. She took it very seriously, while most of the other girls, like Blair, were only taking Film as a break from Advanced Placement hell—AP Calculus, AP Bio, AP History, AP English Literature, AP French. They were on the straight and narrow path to Yale or Harvard or Brown, where their families had all gone for generations. Vanessa wasn't like them. Her parents hadn't even gone to college. They were artists, and Vanessa wanted only one thing in life: to go to NYU and major in film.

Actually, she wanted something else. Or some*one* else, to be precise, but we'll get to that in a minute.

Vanessa was an anomaly at Constance, the only girl in the school who had a nearly shaved head, wore black turtlenecks every day, read Tolstoy's *War and Peace* over and over like it was the Bible, listened to Belle and Sebastian, and drank unsweetened black tea. She had no friends at all at Constance, and lived in Williamsburg, Brooklyn, with her twenty-two-year-old sister, Ruby. So what was she doing at a tiny, exclusive private girls' school on the Upper East Side with princesses like Blair Waldorf? It was a question Vanessa asked herself every day.

Vanessa's parents were older, revolutionary artists who lived in a house made out of recycled car tires in Vermont. When she turned fifteen, they had allowed the perpetually unhappy Vanessa to move in with her bass guitarist older sister in Brooklyn. But they wanted to be sure she got a good, safe, high-school education, so they made her go to Constance.

Vanessa hated it, but she never said anything to her parents. There were only eight months left until graduation. Eight more months and she would finally escape downtown to NYU.

Eight more months of bitchy Blair Waldorf, and even worse, Serena van der Woodsen, who was back in all her splendor. Blair Waldorf looked like she was absolutely orgasmic over the return of her best friend. In fact, the whole back row of Film Studies was atwitter, passing notes tucked into the sleeves of their annoying cashmere sweaters.

Well, fuck them. Vanessa lifted her chin and went on with her presentation. She was above their petty bullshit. *Only eight more months.*

Perhaps if Vanessa had seen the note Kati Farkas had just passed to Blair, she might have had a tad more sympathy for Serena.

> *Dear Blair,*
>   *Can I borrow fifty thousand dollars? Sniff, sniff, sniff. If I don't pay my coke dealer the money I owe him, I'm in big trouble.*
>   *Shit, my crotch itches.*
>   *Let me know about the money.*
> *Love,*
> *Serena v.d. Woodsen*

Blair, Rain, and Kati giggled noisily.

"Shhssh," Mr. Beckham whispered, glancing at Vanessa sympathetically.

Blair turned the note over and scrawled a reply.

> *Sure, Serena. Whatever you want. Call me from jail.*
> *I hear the food is really good there. Nate and I will visit*
> *you whenever we're free, which might be . . . I don't*
> *know . . . NEVER?!*
> *I hope the VD gets better soon.*
> *Love,*
> *Blair*

Blair handed the note back to Kati, feeling only the tiniest speck of remorse for being so mean. There were so many stories about Serena flying around, she honestly didn't know what to believe anymore. Plus, Serena still hadn't actually told anyone what she was doing back, so why should Blair say anything in her defense? Maybe some of it was true. Maybe some of this stuff had really happened.

Besides, passing notes is so much more fun than taking them.

"So I'm going to be writing, directing, and filming this. And I've already cast my friend, Daniel Humphrey, from Riverside Prep, as Prince Andrei," Vanessa explained. Her cheeks heated up when she uttered Dan's name. "But I still need a Natasha for the scene. I'm casting her tomorrow after school, in Madison Square Park at dusk. Anyone interested?" she asked.

The question was a private little joke with herself. Vanessa knew no one in the room was even listening to her; they were too busy passing notes.

Blair's arm shot up. "I'll be the director!" she announced. Obviously she hadn't heard the question, but Blair was so desperate to impress the admissions office at Yale, she was always the first to volunteer for anything.

Vanessa opened her mouth to speak. *Direct this,* she wanted to say, giving Blair the finger.

"Put your hand down, Blair," Mr. Beckham sighed tiredly. "Vanessa just got through telling us *she* is directing and writing and filming. Unless you'd like to try out for the part of Natasha, I suggest you focus on your own project."

Blair glared sourly at him. She hated teachers like Mr. Beckham. He had such a chip on his shoulder because he was from Nebraska and had finally attained his sad dream of living in New York City only to find himself teaching a useless class instead of directing cutting edge films and becoming famous.

"Whatever," Blair said, tucking her dark hair behind her ears. "I guess I really don't have time."

And she didn't.

Blair was chair of the Social Services Board and ran the French Club; she tutored third graders in reading; she worked in a soup kitchen one night a week, had SAT prep on Tuesdays, and on Thursday afternoons she took a fashion design course with Oscar de la Renta. On weekends she played tennis so she could keep up her national ranking. Besides all that, she was on the planning committee of every social function anyone would be bothered to go to, and the fall/winter calendar was *busy, busy, busy.* Her PalmPilot was always running out of memory.

Vanessa flicked on the lights and walked back to her seat at the front of the room.

"It's okay, Blair, I wanted a blond girl for Natasha anyway," she said. Vanessa smoothed her uniform around her thighs and sat down daintily, in an almost perfect imitation of Blair.

Blair smirked at Vanessa's prickly shaved head and glanced at Mr. Beckham, who cleared his throat and stood up. He was hungry, and the bell was going to ring in five minutes.

"Well, that's it, girls. You can leave a little early today.

Vanessa, why don't you put up a sign-up sheet in the hall for your casting tomorrow?"

The girls began to pack up their bags and file out of the room. Vanessa ripped a blank sheet of paper out of her notebook and wrote the necessary details at the top of it. *War and Peace. Short film. Try out for Natasha. Wednesday P.M., sunset. Madison Square Park. Park bench, Northeast corner.* She resisted writing an exact description of the girl she was looking for, because she didn't want to scare anyone away. But she had a clear picture in her mind, and it wasn't going to be easy to find the right girl.

Her perfect Natasha would be pale and blond, a natural dirty blond. She wouldn't be too obviously pretty, but she'd have the kind of face that made you want to look at it. She would be the kind of girl to make Dan glow—full of movement and laughter—exactly the opposite of Dan's quiet energy, which burned deep inside him and made his hands shake sometimes.

Vanessa hugged herself. Just thinking about Dan made her feel like she had to pee. Under that shaved head and that impossible black turtleneck, she was just a girl.

Face it: we're all the same.

a power lunch

"The invitations, the gift bags, and the champagne. That's all we have left to do," Blair said. She lifted a cucumber slice off her plate and nibbled at it thoughtfully. "Kate Spade is still doing the gift bags, but I don't know—do you think Kate Spade is too boring?"

"I think Kate Spade is perfect," Isabel said, winding her dark hair into a knot on top of her head. "I mean, think how cool it is to have a plain black handbag now instead of all those animal prints and military shit everyone has. It's all such . . . *bad taste*, don't you think?"

Blair nodded. "Completely," she agreed.

"Hey, what about my leopard skin coat?" Kati said, looking hurt.

"Yes, but that's *real* leopard skin," Blair argued. "That's different."

The three girls were sitting in the Constance cafeteria, discussing the upcoming *Kiss on the Lips* benefit to raise money for the Central Park Peregrine Falcon Foundation. Blair was chair of the organizing committee, of course.

"Those poor birds," Blair sighed.

As if she could give two shits about the damned birds.

"I really want this party to be good," she said. "You guys are coming to my meeting tomorrow, right?"

"Of course we're coming," Isabel said. "What about Serena—did you tell her about the party? Is she going to help?"

Blair stared blankly back at her.

Kati wrinkled her pert little ski-jump nose and nudged Isabel with her elbow. "I bet Serena is too busy, you know, dealing with everything. All her *problems*. She probably doesn't have time to help us, anyway," she said, smirking.

Blair shrugged. Across the cafeteria, Serena herself was just joining the lunch line. She noticed Blair right away and smiled, waving cheerfully as if to say, "I'll be there in a minute!" Blair blinked, pretending she'd forgotten to put in her contacts.

Serena slid her tray along the metal counter, choosing a lemon yogurt and skipping all the hot lunch selections until she came to the hot-water dispenser, where she filled up a cup with hot water and placed a Lipton tea bag, a slice of lemon, and a packet of sugar on the saucer. Then she carried her tray over to the salad bar, where she filled up a plate with a pile of romaine lettuce and poured a small puddle of bleu cheese dressing beside it. She would have preferred a toasted ham-and-cheese sandwich in the Gare du Nord in Paris, eaten in a hurry before leaping onto her London train, but this was almost as good. It was the same lunch she'd eaten at Constance every day since sixth grade. Blair always got the same thing too. They called it the "diet plate."

Blair watched as Serena got her salad, dreading the moment when Serena would sit down next to her in all her glory and start trying to be friends again. Ugh.

"Hey guys," Serena said, sitting down next to Blair, smiling radiantly. "Just like old times, huh?" She laughed and peeled back the top of her yogurt. The cuffs of her brother's old shirt were frayed, and stray threads dangled in the yogurt's watery whey.

"Hello, Serena," Kati and Isabel said in unison.

Blair looked up at Serena and turned the corners of her glossy lips upwards. It was almost a smile.

Serena stirred the yogurt up and nodded at Blair's tray, where the remains of her bagel with cream cheese and cucumber were strewn. "I guess you outgrew the diet plate," she observed.

"I guess," Blair said. She smashed a lump of cream cheese into her paper napkin with her thumb, staring at Serena's sloppy cuffs in bewilderment. It was fine to wear your brother's old clothes in ninth and tenth grade. Then, it was cool. But now? It just seemed . . . *dirty*.

"So my schedule totally sucks," Serena said, licking her spoon. "I don't have a single class with you guys."

"Um, that's because you're not taking any APs," Kati observed.

"You're lucky," Isabel sighed. "I have so much work to do I don't even have time to sleep."

"Well, at least I'll have more time to party," Serena said. She nudged Blair's elbow. "What's going on this month, anyway? I feel so completely out of it."

Blair sat up straight and picked up her plastic cup, only to find there was no water left in it to drink. She knew she should tell Serena all about the *Kiss on the Lips* party and how Serena could help with the preparations and how fun it was all going to be. But somehow she couldn't bring herself to do it. Serena was out of it, all right. And Blair wanted her to stay that way.

"It's been pretty lame. There really isn't much going on until Christmas," Blair lied, shooting a warning glance at Kati and Isabel.

"Really?" Serena said, disappointed. "Well what about tonight? You guys want to go out?"

Blair glanced at her friends. She was all for going out, but it was only Tuesday. The most she ever did on a Tuesday night was rent a movie with Nate. Suddenly Blair felt seriously old and boring. Leave it to Serena to make her feel boring.

"I have an AP French test tomorrow. Sorry, Serena," Blair said. She stood up. "Actually, I have a meeting with Madame Rogers right now."

Serena frowned and began to chew on her thumbnail, a new habit she'd picked up at boarding school. "Well, maybe I'll give Nate a call. He'll go out with me," she said.

Blair picked up her tray and resisted hurling it in Serena's face. *Keep your hands off him!* she wanted to scream, jumping onto the table ninja-style. *Hiyeeh-yah!*

"I'll see you later, guys," she said, and walked stiffly away.

Serena sighed and flicked a piece of lettuce off her plate. Blair was being boring. When were they going to start having fun? She looked up at Kati and Isabel hopefully, but they were getting ready to leave, too.

"I've got a stupid college advisor meeting," Kati said.

"And I have to go up to the art room and put my painting away," Isabel said.

"Before anyone sees it?" Kati joked.

"Oh, shut up," Isabel said.

They stood up with their trays.

"It's so good to have you back, Serena," Kati said in her fakest voice.

"Yeah," Isabel agreed. "It really is."

And then they walked away.

Serena twirled her spoon around and around in her yogurt container, wondering what had happened to everyone. They were all acting like freaks. *What did I do?* she asked herself, chewing on her thumbnail again.

Good question.

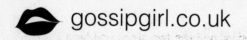

Disclaimer: All the real names of places, people, and events have been altered or abbreviated to protect the innocent. Namely, me.

hey people!

WHERE THE BOYS ARE

Thanks for checking in, although most of you had little to say about *S* or *B*. Most of you just want to know more about the boys.

Your E-mail:

Q: Dear gg,
D sounds sweet. Whats he so hot for *S* for? Shes just a ho.
—Bebe

A: Dear Bebe,
I happen to know that *D* is not that innocent. He was up to some kinky shit back at summer camp in eighth grade.
—GG

Q: dear GG,
what does *N* do at lunchtime?? i go to school near him, and i wonder if i see him all the time without realizing it. Yikes!
—ShyGirl

Okay, if you want to know so badly, then I'll tell you.

St. Jude's lets its senior boys out for lunch. So right now *N* is probably headed up to that little pizza joint on the corner of Eightieth and Madison. Vino's? Vinnie's? Whatever. Anyway, they have good slices and one of the delivery guys sells pretty decent pot. *N* is one of his regulars. There's usually a group of kids from L'Ecole standing around outside the pizza place, so *N* will stop and flirt with this one girl who I'll call *Claire*, who acts all shy and pretends she doesn't speak English, but she's actually really bad at French and a huge slut.

N has this cute little gag where he buys two slices and he always offers *Claire* one. She holds onto it the whole time they're talking and finally takes a little weeny bit off the tip of the slice. Then *N* goes, "I can't believe you did that, you're eating my pizza!" and swipes the thing out of her hands and eats the whole thing in like two bites. This makes *Claire* laugh so hard her boobs nearly pop out of her shirt. The L'Ecole girls all wear really tight clothes and short skirts and high heels. They're like, the ho's of the Upper East Side school system. *N* likes to flirt with them, and so far that's as far as it's gone. But if *B* leads him on any longer, he might start giving *Claire* more than just a bite of his pizza. This time, though, *Claire* surprises him by asking if he's heard about *S*. *Claire* claims to have heard that *S* not only got pregnant last year, but that she gave birth in France. Her baby's name is *Jules* and he is alive and well and living in Marseilles.

As for *D*—well, he's sitting outside in the Riverside Prep courtyard again, reading poetry and eating PB and J. I know that sounds extremely sad, but don't worry about *D*. His time is coming. Stay tuned.

Sightings

K was seen returning a pink, army-print handbag at **Barneys**. Personally, I thought the bag was cute. But someone must have talked her out of it.

You know you love me,

gossip girl

messages

"Hey Nate. It's Serena. I'm just calling to see what you're up to. I thought maybe we could go out tonight, but you know what? I'm tired. It's only ten, but I think I'm going to bed. I'll see you this weekend though, okay? I can't wait. Love you. Nighty-night."

Serena hung up. Her room felt very quiet. Even Fifth Avenue was still, except for the occasional passing taxi.

From where she sat on her big canopy bed, she could see the silver-framed photograph of her family, taken in Greece when she was twelve. The captain of the sailboat they'd chartered had taken the picture. They were all in bathing suits, and her brother, Erik, who was fourteen at the time, was making a big fart kiss on Serena's cheek while their parents looked on, laughing. Serena had gotten her period for the first time on that trip. She'd been so embarrassed, she couldn't bear to tell her parents, but what was she supposed to do, trapped on a boat? They were anchored off the island of Rhodes, and while their parents were snorkeling and Serena and Erik were supposed to be having windsurfing lessons, Erik had swum ashore, stolen a Vespa, and bought her some maxi pads. He came back with them in a little plastic bag, tied on top of his head, her hero.

Serena had thrown her ruined underwear overboard. They were probably still there, stuck on a reef somewhere.

Now Erik was a freshman at Brown, and Serena never got to see him. He had been in France with her that summer, but they'd both spent the whole time chasing or being chased by boys and girls, so they'd never really had time to talk.

Serena picked up the phone again and pressed the speed-dial button for her brother's off-campus apartment. The phone rang and rang until finally the voicemail system picked up.

ge for Drew, press three. If you would like to leave a message for Erik, press four."

Serena pressed four and then hesitated. " . . . Hey . . . Hey . . . it's Serena. Sorry I haven't called in a while. But you could have called me too, you big jerk. I was stuck up in Ridgefield, bored out of my mind, until this weekend, and now I'm back in the city. I had my first day of school today. It was kind of strange. Actually it sucked. Everyone is . . . everything is . . . I don't know . . . it's weird. . . . Anyway, call me. I miss your hairy ass. I'll send you a care-package as soon as I get a chance. Love you. Bye."

life is fragile and absurd

"You're so full of shit, Dan," Jenny Humphrey told her brother. They were sitting at the kitchen table in their large and crumbling tenth-floor, four-bedroom West End Avenue apartment. It was a beautiful old place with twelve-foot ceilings, lots of sunny windows, big walk-in closets, and huge bathtubs with feet, but it hadn't been renovated since the 1940s. The walls were waterstained and cracked, and the wood floors were scratched and dull. Ancient, mammoth dust bunnies had gathered in the corners and along the baseboards like moss. Once in a while Jenny and Dan's father, Rufus Humphrey, hired a cleaning service to scrub the place down, and their enormous cat, Marx, kept the cockroaches in order, but most of the time their home felt like a cozy, neglected attic. It was the kind of place where you'd expect to find lost treasures like ancient photographs, vintage shoes, or a bone from last year's Christmas dinner.

Jenny was eating half a grapefruit and drinking a cup of peppermint tea. Ever since she'd gotten her period last spring, she'd been eating less and less. Everything she ate went straight to her boobs, anyway. Dan worried about his little sister's eating habits, but Jenny was as spunky and energetic as ever, so what did he know? For instance, he didn't know that Jenny bought a toasted, buttered, chocolate-chip scone almost every day on her way to school at a little gourmet deli on Broadway.

Not exactly a great strategy for breast reduction.

Dan was eating an Entenmann's chocolate donut—his second—and sipping instant coffee with Coffee-mate and four teaspoons of sugar. He liked sugar and caffeine, which was probably part of the reason why his hands shook. Dan wasn't into being healthy. He liked to live on the edge.

While he ate, Dan was studying Vanessa Abrams's script for her short film, the film he was supposed to star in. He kept reading the same line, over and over, like a mantra: *Life is fragile and absurd.*

"Tell me you don't care about Serena van der Woodsen being back," Jenny challenged Dan. She put a piece of grapefruit in her mouth and sucked on it. Then she stuck her fingers in her mouth, pulled out the white pulpy skin stuff, and put it on her plate. "You should see her," she went on. "She looks so completely cool. It's like she has this whole new look. I don't mean her clothes; it's her face. She looks older, but it's not like wrinkles or anything. It's like she's Kate Moss or some model who's like, been everywhere and seen everything and come out on the other side. She looks like she's totally, like, *experienced*."

Jenny waited for her brother to respond, but he was just staring into his coffee cup.

Life is fragile and absurd.

"Don't you even want to see her?" Jenny asked.

Dan thought about what he'd heard Chuck Bass say about Serena. He hadn't wanted to believe any of it, but if Serena looked as experienced as Jenny said, maybe what Chuck said was true. Maybe Serena really was the sluttiest, druggiest, most venereally diseased girl in New York.

Dan shrugged his shoulders and pointed at the pile of grapefruit carcasses on Jenny's plate. "That is so foul," he said. "Can't you just eat a Pop-Tart or something, like a normal person?"

"What's wrong with grapefruit?" Jenny said. "It's refreshing."

"Watching you eat it like that isn't. It's disgusting," Dan said. He stuffed the rest of his donut in his mouth and licked the chocolate off his fingers, being careful not to smudge any on his script.

"Don't look, then," said Jenny. "Anyway, you didn't answer my question."

Dan looked up. "What question?"

Jenny put her elbows on the table and leaned forward. "About Serena," she said. "I know you want to see her."

Dan looked back down at his script and shrugged. "Whatever," he said.

"Yeah, whatever," said Jenny, rolling her eyes. "Look, there's this party the Friday after next. It's some big fancy benefit thing to save the peregrine falcons that live in Central Park. Did you know there were falcons in Central Park? I didn't. Anyway, Blair Waldorf is organizing it, and you know she and Serena are best friends, so of course Serena will be there."

Dan kept reading his script, completely ignoring his sister. And Jenny went on, ignoring the fact that Dan was ignoring her.

"Anyway, all we have to do is find a way to get into that party," Jenny said. She grabbed a paper napkin off the table, scrunched it into a ball, and threw it at her brother's head. "Dan, please," she said pleadingly. "We have to go!"

Dan tossed the script aside and looked at his sister, his brown eyes serious and sad.

"Jenny," he said. "I don't want to go to that party. Next Friday night I'm probably going over to Deke's house to use his PlayStation, and then I'll probably head over to Brooklyn to hang out with Vanessa and her sister and their friends. Just like I do every Friday night."

Jenny kicked at the legs of her chair like a little girl. "But why, Dan? Why won't you go to the party?"

Dan shook his head, smiling bitterly. "Because we weren't invited? Because we're not *going* to be invited? Give it up, Jen. I'm sorry, but that's just the way it is. We're different from them, you know that. We don't live in the same world as Serena van der Woodsen or Blair Waldorf or any of those people."

"Oh, you're such a wimp! You drive me crazy," Jen said, rolling her eyes. She stood up and dumped her dishes in the sink, scrubbing at them furiously with a Brillo pad. Then she whirled around and put her hands on her hips. She was wearing a pink flannel nightshirt and her curly brown hair was sticking out all over because she had gone to sleep with it wet. She looked like a mini disgruntled housewife with boobs that were ten times too big for her body.

"I don't care what you say. I'm going to that party!" she insisted.

"What party?" their father asked, appearing in the doorway to the kitchen.

If there were an award for the most embarrassing dad in the universe, Rufus Humphrey would have won it. He was wearing a sweat-stained white wife-beater and red checked boxer shorts, and was scratching at his crotch. He hadn't shaved in a few days, and his gray beard seemed to be growing at different intervals. Some of it was thick and long, but in between were bald patches and patches of five o'clock shadow. His curly gray hair was matted and his brown eyes bleary. There was a cigarette tucked behind each of his ears.

Jenny and Dan looked at their father for a moment in silence.

Then Jenny sighed and turned back to the dishes. "Never mind," she said.

Dan smirked and leaned back in his chair. Their father hated the Upper East Side and all its pretensions. He only sent Jenny to Constance because it was a very good school and because he used to date one of the English teachers there. But he hated the idea that Jenny might be influenced by her classmates, or "those *debutantes*," as he called them.

Dan knew their dad was going to love this.

"Jenny wants to go to some fancy benefit next week," he said.

Mr. Humphrey pulled one of the cigarettes from behind his ear and stuck it in his mouth, playing with it between his lips. "A benefit for what?" he demanded.

Dan rocked his chair back and forth, a smug look on his face. Jenny turned off the faucet and glared at him, daring him to go on.

"Get this," Dan said. "It's a party to raise money for those peregrine falcons that live in Central Park. They're probably going to build like, birdhouse mansions for them or something. Like there aren't thousands of homeless people that could use the money."

"Oh, shut up," Jenny said, furious. "You think you know everything. It's just a stupid party. I never said it was a great cause."

"You call that a *cause*?" her father bellowed. "Shame on you. Those people only want those birds around because they're *pretty*. Because it makes them feel like they're in the pretty *countryside*, like they're at their houses in *Connecticut* or *Maine*. They're *decorative*. Leave it to the leisure class to come up with some charity that does absolutely *no one* any good at all!"

Jenny leaned back against the kitchen counter, stared up at the ceiling, and tuned her father out. She'd heard this same tirade before. It didn't change anything. She still wanted to go to that party.

"I just want to have some fun," she said stubbornly. "Why does it have to be such a big deal?"

"It's a big deal because you're going to get used to this silly debutante nonsense, and you're going to wind up a big fake like your mother, who hangs around rich people all the time because she's too scared to think for herself," her father shouted, his unshaven face turning dark red. "Dammit, Jenny. You remind me more and more of your mother every day."

Dan suddenly felt bad.

Their mother had run off to Prague with some count or prince or something, and she was basically a kept woman, letting the count or prince or whatever he was dress her and put her up in hotels all over Europe. All she did all day was shop, eat, drink, and paint pictures of flowers. She wrote them letters a few times a year, and sent them the odd present. Last Christmas she'd sent Jenny a peasant dress from Germany. It was about ten sizes too small.

It wasn't a nice thing for their father to say that Jenny reminded him of their mother. It wasn't nice at all.

Jenny looked like she was about to cry.

"Lay off, Dad," Dan said. "We weren't invited to the party anyway. So neither of us could go even if we wanted to."

"See what I mean!" Mr. Humphrey said triumphantly. "Why would you want to hang out with those snobs anyway?"

Jenny stared glassy-eyed at the dirty kitchen floor.

Dan stood up. "Hurry up and get dressed, Jen," he said gently. "I'll walk you to your bus stop."

n gets an e-vitation

In the six-minute interval between the bell signaling the end of Latin and the bell signaling the beginning of Gym, Nate slipped into the computer lab at the St. Jude's School for Boys. Every Wednesday, he and Blair had grown accustomed to e-mailing each other a quick love note (okay, it was Blair's idea), to help them get over the hump of the boring school week. Only two more days until the weekend, when they could spend as much time together as they wanted.

But today Nate wasn't even thinking of Blair. He wanted to see how Serena was doing. Last night she had left a message on the answering machine in his room while he was watching a Yankees game with his friends. Her voice had sounded lonely and sad and very far away, even though she lived only a block and a half away from him. Nate had never heard Serena sound so down. And since when did Serena van der Woodsen go to bed early?

Nate sat down in front of one of the humming PCs in the lab. He clicked on the New Mail window and typed a message to Serena's old Constance e-mail address. He didn't know if she would check it or not, but it was worth a try.

```
TO: serenavdw@constancebillard.edu
FROM: narchibald@stjudes.edu

Hey. What are you up to? I got your mes-
sage last night. Sorry I wasn't there. I
will definitely see you Friday, okay?
Love, Nate.
```

Then he opened up his own e-mail. Surprise, surprise, there
was a note from Blair. They hadn't talked since her mother's
party the night before last.

```
TO: narchibald@stjudes.edu
FROM: blairw@constancebillard.edu

Dear Nate.
I miss you. Monday night was supposed to be
really special. Before we got interrupted I
was planning for us to do something we've
been talking about doing for a while. I
think you know what I'm talking about. The
timing wasn't right, I guess. I just wanted
to tell you that I'm ready to do it. I
wasn't ready before, but now I am. My Mom
and Cyrus are going away on Friday and I
really want you to sleep over.
I love you. Call me.
          Love,
          Blair.
```

Nate read Blair's e-mail twice and then closed the file so he
wouldn't have to look at it anymore. It was only Wednesday. Was

it possible that Blair could remain ignorant about him and Serena until Friday, even though she was in school with Serena every day and they were best friends and told each other everything? Chances were, no. And what about Chuck Bass? He wasn't exactly good at keeping secrets.

Nate rubbed his pretty green eyes viciously. It didn't matter how Blair found out. Any way he looked at it, he was fucked. He tried to come up with a plan, but the only plan he could think of was to wait and see what happened when he saw Blair on Friday night. There was no point in getting all worked up about it now.

Just then the door to the computer lab opened, and Jeremy Scott Tompkinson poked his head around the door.

"Yo, Nathaniel, we're cutting Gym. Come to the park with us and play some ball."

The second bell rang. Nate was late for Gym anyway, and after Gym he had lunch. Cutting sounded like an excellent idea.

"Yeah, sure," Nate said. "Hold on a sec." He clicked on Blair's e-mail and dragged it across the screen and into the trash. "Okay," he said, standing up. "Let's go."

Hmmm, if he really loved her, he probably would've saved the e-mail, or at least answered it, right?

It was a sunny October day in Central Park. Out in Sheep Meadow lots of kids were cutting school, just lying in the grass, smoking, or playing Frisbee. The trees surrounding the meadow were a blaze of yellows, oranges, and reds, and beyond the trees loomed the beautiful old apartment buildings on Central Park West. A guy was selling weed, and Anthony Avuldsen bought some to add to what Nate had picked up at the pizza place yesterday at lunch. Nate, Jeremy, Anthony, and Charlie Dern passed an enormous joint between them as they dribbled a soccer ball around on the grass.

Charlie puffed on the joint and passed it to Jeremy. Nate shot him the ball and Charlie tripped over it. He was six feet tall, and his head was too big for his body. People called him Frankenstein. Ever the blond athletic one, even when he was stoned, Anthony dove for the ball, kicked it up in the air and headed it at Jeremy. It hit Jeremy in his puny chest and he let it roll to the ground, dribbling it between his feet.

"Shit, this stuff is strong," Jeremy said, hitching up his pants. They were always sliding down below his skinny hips, no matter how tightly he buckled his belt.

"Yeah, it is," Nate agreed. "I'm all fucked up." His feet were itchy. It felt like the grass was growing through the rubber soles of his sneakers.

Jeremy stopped dribbling the ball. "Hey, Nate. Have you seen Serena van der Woodsen yet?" he asked. "I heard she's back."

Nate looked at the ball longingly, wishing he had it so he could dribble it away across the field and pretend he hadn't heard Jeremy's question. He could feel the other three boys staring at him. He bent down and pulled his left shoe off so he could scratch the bottom of his foot. Damn, it itched. "Yeah, I saw her Monday," he said casually, hopping up and down on one foot.

Charlie cleared his throat and spit in the grass. "What'd she look like?" he asked. "I heard she got into all sorts of trouble up at Hanover."

"Me too," Anthony said, sucking on the roach. "I heard she got kicked out for having sex with this whole group of guys in her room. Her roommate ratted her out." He laughed. "Like, couldn't she afford a hotel room?"

Charlie laughed. "I heard she has a kid. I'm serious. She had it in France and left it there. Her parents are paying to have it raised in some fancy French convent. It's like a fucking movie, man."

Nate couldn't believe what he was hearing. He dropped his shoe and sat down in the grass. Then he took off his other shoe and pulled off both of his socks. He didn't say anything, he just sat there, scratching his bare feet.

"Can you imagine Serena with all these guys in her dorm room? Like, *Ooh, baby. Harder, harder*!" Jeremy fell down on the grass, rubbing his skinny belly and cackling hysterically. "Oh, man!"

"Wonder if she even knows who the daddy is," Anthony said.

"I heard there was a pretty major drug thing going on, too," Charlie said. "She was dealing and got addicted to whatever it was. She was in rehab in Switzerland all summer. After the baby was born, I guess."

"Whoa, that is fucked up," Jeremy said.

"You and her had a thing, didn't you, Nate?" Charlie said.

"Where'd you hear that?" Nate asked, frowning.

Charlie shook his head and smiled. "I don't know, man. Around. What's the problem? She's hot."

"Yeah, well, I've had hotter," Nate said, and immediately regretted it. What was he *talking* about?

"Yeah, Blair's pretty hot too, I guess," Charlie said.

"I bet she gets pretty crazy in bed," Jeremy agreed.

"Dude's tired just thinking about it!" Anthony said, pointing at Nate and cackling.

Nate laughed and shook his head, trying to shake their words out of his ears. He lay back in the grass and stared at the empty blue sky. If he tilted his head all the way back, he could just see the rooftops of the penthouses along Fifth Avenue, Serena's and Blair's included. Nate let his chin fall so all he could see was blue sky again. He was too baked to deal with any of this. He tuned his friends out and tried to clear his mind completely, his head as empty and blue as the sky. But he couldn't get the images of Serena and Blair out of his mind's eye, floating naked above his head. "You know you love me," they were saying. Nate smiled and closed his eyes.

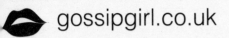
Disclaimer: All the real names of places, people, and events have been altered or abbreviated to protect the innocent. Namely, me.

hey people!

I know it hasn't been long. But I can't resist writing more about **N**. My new favorite topic. He is so stunningly beautiful, after all. Even if he is kind of lacking in the balls department.

STONED IN CENTRAL PARK

Actually, my new favorite topic is the Waspoid—the elite version of the wasteoid, or stoner boy. Unlike the average stoner wasteoid, the Waspoid isn't into metal or online dungeon games or skateboarding or eating vegan. He gets cute haircuts and has good skin. He smells nice, he wears the cashmere sweaters his girlfriend buys for him, he gets decent grades, and he's sweet to his mom. He sails and plays soccer. He knows how to tie a necktie. He knows how to dance. He's sexy! But the Waspoid never fully invests himself in anything or anyone. He isn't a go-getter and he never says what's on his mind. He doesn't take risks, which is what makes it so risky to fall in love with him.

You might have noticed that I'm just the opposite—I never know when to shut up! And I seriously believe that opposites attract. I have to confess, I'm becoming a Waspoid groupie.

Apparently I'm not the only one.

Your E-mail

Dear Gossip Girl,
i hooked up majorly with **N** on a blanket in central park. at least, i think it's the same **N**. he's all freckley, right? does he smell like suntan lotion and weed?
—blanketbaby

A: Dear blanketbaby,
Hmmm. I bet he does.
—GG

Sightings

B buying condoms at **Zitomer** Pharmacy. Lifestyles Extra-Long Super-Ribbed! What I want to know is how she knew what size to get. I guess they've done everything *but*. Afterwards, **B** made a beeline (no pun intended!) to the **J. Sisters** salon for her first Brazilian bikini wax. Ouch. But believe me, it's worth it. Also caught **S** at the post office, mailing a big package. Barneys baby clothes for her little French tot, maybe? Caught **I** and **K** in the **3 Guys Coffee Shop**, eating fries and hot cocoa again. They'd just returned those cute little dresses they bought at Bendel's the other day—oh dear, are they getting too fat?—and were discussing other options for what to wear to the *Kiss on the Lips* party. Too bad it's not a toga party.

Vocab

Since so many of you have been asking, I'm going to answer the big question that's been baffling you since you found out about the party for the peregrine falcons.

Okay. According to my handy unabridged dictionary:

<u>Falcon</u>, n. 1. any of several birds of prey of the family Falconidae, esp. of the genus Falco, usually distinguished by long, pointed wings, a hooked beak with a tooth-like notch on each side of the upper bill, and swift agile flight, typically diving to seize prey: some falcon species are close to extinction. <u>Peregrine</u> <u>falcon</u>, a globally distributed falcon, *Falco perigrinus*, much used in falconry because of its swift flight.

I'm sure I had you on the edge of your seat about that one. But I'm just trying to keep you in the know—that's my job.

See you in the park!

You know you love me,

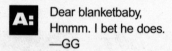

s tries to improve herself

"Well, it's wonderful to have you back, dear," Ms. Glos, Constance's college advisor, told Serena. She picked her glasses up from where they were hanging around her neck on a gold chain and slid them onto her nose so she could examine Serena's schedule, which was lying on her desk. "Let's see, now. Mmmm. Yes. Right," she muttered, reading the schedule over.

Serena sat in front of Ms. Glos, with her legs crossed, waiting patiently. There were no diplomas on Ms. Glos's wall, no evidence of any accreditations at all, just pictures of her grandchildren. Serena wondered if Ms. Glos had even gone to college. You would have thought that if she were going to dish out advice on the subject, she could have at least tried it.

Ms. Glos cleared her throat. "Yes, well, your schedule is perfectly acceptable. Not stellar, mind you, but adequate. I imagine you're making up for it with extracurriculars, yes?"

Serena shrugged her shoulders. *If you can call drinking Pernod and dancing naked on a beach in Cannes an extracurricular.* "Not really," she said. "I mean, I'm not actually signed up for any extracurriculars at the moment."

Ms. Glos let her glasses drop. Her nostrils were turning very red and Serena wondered if she was about to have a bloody nose. Ms. Glos was famous for her bloody noses. Her skin was very pale, with a yellowish tinge. All the girls thought she had some terrible contagious disease.

"No extracurriculars? But what are you doing to improve yourself?"

Serena gave Ms. Glos a polite, blank look.

Who said she needed improving?

"I see. Well, we'll have to get you involved in *something*, won't we?" Ms. Glos said. "I'm afraid the colleges aren't going to even look at you without any extracurriculars." She bent over and pulled a big looseleaf binder out of a drawer in her desk and began flipping through pages and pages of flyers printed on colored paper. "Here's something that starts this week. 'Feng Shui Flowers, the Art of Floral Design.'"

She looked up at Serena, who was frowning doubtfully. "No, you're right. That's not going to get you into Harvard, is it?" Ms. Glos said with a little laugh.

She pushed up the sleeves of her blouse and frowned at the binder as she flipped briskly through the pages. She wasn't about to give up after only one try. She was very good at her job.

Serena gnawed on her thumbnail. She hadn't thought about this. That colleges would actually need her to be anything more than she already was. And she definitely wanted to go to college. A good one. Her parents certainly expected her to go to one of the best schools. Not that they put any pressure on her—but it went without saying. And the more Serena thought about it, the more she realized she really didn't have *anything* going for her. She'd been kicked out of boarding school, her grades had fallen, she had no idea what was going on in any of her classes, and she had no hobbies or cool after-school activities. Her SAT scores sucked because her mind always wandered during those stupid fill-in-the-bubble tests. And when she took them again, they would probably suck even worse. Basically, she was screwed.

"What about drama? Your English grades are quite good, you must like drama," Ms. Glos suggested. "They've only been rehearsing this one for a little over a week. It's the Interschool Drama Club doing a modern version of *Gone With the Wind*." She looked up again. "How 'bout it?"

Serena jiggled her foot up and down and chewed on her pinky nail. She tried to imagine herself alone on stage playing Scarlett O'Hara. She would have to cry on cue, and pretend to faint, and wear huge dresses with corsets and hoop skirts. Maybe even a wig.

I'll never go hungry again! she'd cry dramatically, in her best Southern-belle voice. It might be kind of fun.

Serena took the flyer from Ms. Glos's hand, careful not to touch the paper where Ms. Glos had touched it.

"Sure, why not?" she said. "It sounds like fun."

Serena left Ms. Glos's office as the final class of the day was getting out. *Gone With the Wind* rehearsal was in the auditorium, but it didn't begin until six so that the students who did sports right after school could still be in the play. Serena walked up Constance's wide central stairwell to the fourth floor to retrieve her coat from her locker and see if anyone wanted to hang out until six. All around her, girls were flying past, a blur of end-of-the-day energy, rushing to their next meeting, practice, rehearsal, or club. Out of habit, they paused for half a second to say hello to Serena, because ever since they could remember, to be seen talking to Serena van der Woodsen was to be *seen*.

"Hey Serena," Laura Salmon yelled before diving down the stairs for Glee Club in the basement music room.

"Later, Serena," Rain Hoffstetter said, as she slipped past in her gym shorts, heading for soccer practice.

"See you tomorrow, Serena," Lily Reed said softly, blushing because she was wearing her riding breeches, which always embarrassed her.

"Bye," Carmen Fortier said, chewing gum in her leather jacket and jeans. She was one of the few scholarship girls in the junior class and lived in the Bronx. She claimed she couldn't wear her uniform home or she'd get beaten up. Carmen was headed to the Art of Floral Design Club, although she always lied to her friends in her neighborhood and said she took karate.

Suddenly the hallway was empty. Serena opened her locker, pulled her Burberry coat off the hook, and put it on. Then she slammed her locker shut and trotted downstairs and out the school doors, turning left down Ninety-third Street toward Central Park.

There was a box of orange Tic Tacs in her pocket with only one Tic Tac left. Serena fished the Tic Tac out and put it on her tongue, but she was so worried about her future, she could barely taste it.

She crossed Fifth Avenue, walking along the sidewalk that bordered the park. Fallen leaves scattered the pavement. Down the block, two little Sacred Heart girls in their cute red-and-white checked pinafores were walking an enormous black Rottweiler. Serena thought about entering the park at Eighty-ninth Street and sitting down for a while to kill time before the play rehearsal. But alone? What would she do, people-watch? She had always been one of those people everyone *else* watches.

So she went home.

Home was 994 Fifth Avenue, a ritzy, white-glove building next to the Stanhope Hotel and directly across the street from the Metropolitan Museum of Art. The van der Woodsens owned half of the top floor. Their apartment had fourteen rooms, including five bedrooms with private bathrooms, a maid's apartment, a ballroom-sized living room, and two seriously cool lounges with wet bars and huge entertainment systems.

When Serena got home the enormous apartment was empty. Her parents were rarely home. Her father ran the same Dutch shipping firm his great-great-grandfather had founded in the 1700s. Both her parents were on the boards of all the big charities and arts organizations in the city and always had meetings or lunches or fundraisers to go to. Deidre, the maid, was out shopping, but the place was spotless and there were vases of fresh cut flowers in every room, including the bathrooms.

Serena slid open the door to the smaller of the lounges and flopped down on her favorite blue velvet armchair. She picked up the remote control and pressed the buttons to open the TV cabinet and turn on the flat-screen TV. She flipped through the channels impatiently, unable to focus on anything she saw, finally settling on *TRL*, even though she thought Carson Daly was the most annoying man alive. She hadn't been watching much TV lately. At boarding school, her dormmates would make popcorn and hot chocolate and watch *Saturday Night Live* or *Jackass* in their pajamas, but Serena preferred to slip away to drink peach schnapps and smoke cigars with the boys in the chapel basement.

But what bothered her most now was not Carson Daly or even the fact that she was sitting alone in her house with nothing to do, but the thought that she might spend the rest of her life doing just that—watching TV alone in her parents' apartment—if she didn't get her act together and get into college! Why was she so stupid? Everyone else seemed to have their shit together. Had she missed the all-important "it's time to get your shit together" talk? Why hadn't anyone warned her?

Well, there was no point in freaking out. She still had time. And she could still have fun. She didn't have to become a nun just because she was joining the Interschool Drama Club, or whatever.

Serena clicked the TV off and wandered into the kitchen. The van der Woodsens' kitchen was massive. Glass cabinets lined the walls above gleaming, stainless-steel counter tops. There were two restaurant stoves and three Sub-Zero refrigerators. An enormous butcher-block table stood in the center of the kitchen, and on the table was today's pile of mail.

Serena picked up the mail and sifted through it. Mostly, there were invitations for her parents—white square envelopes printed with old-fashioned typefaces—to balls, benefit dinners, fundraisers, and auctions. Then there were the art openings—postcards with a picture of the artist's work on one side and the details of the opening on the back. One of these caught Serena's eye. It had obviously been lost in the mail for a little while, because it looked beaten up, and the opening it announced was beginning at 4 P.M. on Wednesday, which was . . . *right now*. Serena flipped the card over and looked at the picture of the artist's work. It looked like a close-up black-and-white photograph of an eye, tinted with pink. The title of the work was *Kate Moss*. And the name of the show was "Behind the Scene." Serena squinted at the picture. There was something innocent and beautiful about it, and at the same time it was a little gross. Maybe it wasn't an eye. She wasn't sure what it was. It was definitely cool, though. There was no question about it; Serena knew what she was doing for the next two hours.

She flew into her bedroom, whipped off her maroon uniform, and pulled on her favorite pair of black leather jeans. Then she grabbed her coat and called the elevator. Within minutes she was stepping out of a taxi in front of the Whitehot Gallery downtown in Chelsea.

The minute she got there, Serena grabbed a free gin martini and signed the guest list. The gallery was full of twenty-something hipsters in cool clothes, drinking free martinis and admiring the photographs hanging on the walls. Each picture was similar to the one on the postcard, that same close-up black-and-white eye, blown up, all in different shapes and sizes and tinted with different colors. Under each one was a label, and on every label was the name of a celebrity: Kate Moss, Kate Hudson, Joaquin Phoenix, Jude Law, Gisele Bundchen, Cher, Eminem, Christina Aguilera, Madonna, Elton John.

French pop music bubbled out of invisible speakers. The photo-artists themselves, the Remi brothers, identical twin sons of a French model and an English duke, were being interviewed and photographed for *Art Forum*, *Vogue*, *W*, *Harper's Bazaar*, and the *New York Times*.

Serena studied each photograph carefully. They weren't eyes, she decided, now that she was looking at them blown up. But what were they? Belly buttons?

Suddenly Serena felt an arm around her waist.

"Hello, *ma chèrie*. Beautiful girl. What is your name?"

It was one of the Remi brothers. He was twenty-six years old and five foot seven, the same height as Serena. He had curly black hair and brilliant blue eyes. He spoke with a French and British accent. He was dressed head to toe in navy blue, and his lips were dark red and curved foxily up at the corners. He was absolutely gorgeous, and so was his twin brother.

Lucky girl.

Serena didn't resist when he pulled her into a photograph

with him and his brother for the *New York Times* Sunday Styles section. One brother stood behind Serena and kissed her neck while the other knelt in front of her and hugged her knees. Around them, people watched greedily, eager to catch a glimpse of the new "it" girl.

Everyone in New York wants to be famous. Or at least see someone who is so they can brag about it later.

The *New York Times* society reporter recognized Serena from parties a year or so back, but he had to be sure it was her. "Serena van der Woodsen, right?" he said, looking up from his notepad.

Serena blushed and nodded. She was used to being recognized.

"You *must* model for us," one of the Remi brothers gasped, kissing Serena's hand.

"You must," the other one agreed, feeding her an olive.

Serena laughed. "Sure," she said. "Why not?" Although she had no idea what she was agreeing to.

One of the Remi brothers pointed to a door marked Private across the gallery. "We'll meet you in there," he said. "Don't be nervous. We're both gay."

Serena giggled and took a big gulp of her drink. Were they kidding?

The other brother patted her on the bottom. "It's all right darling. You're absolutely stunning, so you've got nothing to worry about. Go on. We'll be there in a minute."

Serena hesitated, but only for a second. She could keep up with the likes of Christina Aguilera and Joaquin Phoenix. No problem. Chin up, she headed for the door marked Private.

Just then, a guy from the Public Arts League and a woman from the New York Transit Authority came over to talk to the Remi brothers about a new avant-garde public art program.

They wanted to put a Remi brothers' photograph on the sides of buses, in subways, and in the advertising boxes on top of taxis all over town.

"Yes, of course," the Remis agreed. "If you can wait a moment, we'll have a brand new one. We can give it to you exclusively!"

"What's this one called?" the Transit Authority woman asked eagerly.

"*Serena*," the Remi boys said in unison.

social awareness is next to godliness

"I found a printer who will do it by tomorrow afternoon and hand deliver each of the invitations so they get there by Friday morning," Isabel said, looking pleased with herself for being so efficient.

"But look how expensive it is. If we use them, then we're going to have to cut costs on other things. See how much Takashimaya is charging us for the flowers?"

As soon as they were finished with their Wednesday after-school activities, the *Kiss on the Lips* organizing committee had convened over French fries and hot chocolate in a booth at the 3 Guys Coffee Shop—Blair, Isabel, Kati, and Tina Ford, from the Seaton Arms School—to deal with the last-minute preparations for the party.

The crisis at hand was the fact that the party was only nine days away, and no one had received an invitation yet. The invitations had been ordered weeks ago, but due to a mix-up the location of the party had to be changed from The Park—a hot new restaurant in lower Chelsea—to the old Barneys building on Seventeenth Street and Seventh Avenue, rendering the invitations useless. The girls were in a tight spot. They had to get a new set of invitations out, and fast, or there wasn't going to be a party at all.

"But Takashimaya is the *only* place to get flowers. And it really doesn't cost much. Oh, come on, Blair, think how cool they'll be," Tina whined.

"Yes, it does," Blair insisted. "And there are plenty of other places to get flowers."

"Well, maybe we can ask the peregrine falcon people to pitch in," Isabel suggested. She reached for a French fry, dunked it in ketchup, and popped it into her mouth. "They've barely done anything."

Blair rolled her eyes, and blew into her hot chocolate. "That's the whole point. *We're* raising money for *them*. It's a *cause*."

Kati wound a lock of her frizzy blond hair around her finger. "What *is* a peregrine falcon anyway?" she said. "Is it like a wood-pecker?"

"No, I think they're bigger," Tina said. "And they eat other animals, you know, like rabbits and mice and stuff."

"Gross," Kati said.

"I just read a definition of what one was the other day," Isabel mused. "I can't remember where I saw it."

gossipgirl.co.uk, perhaps?

"They're almost extinct," Blair added. She thumbed through the list of people they were inviting to the party. There were three hundred and sixteen all together. All young people—no parents, thank God.

Blair's eyes were automatically drawn to a name toward the bottom of the list: Serena van der Woodsen. The address given was her dorm room at Hanover Academy, in New Hampshire. Blair put the list back down on the table without correcting Serena's address.

"We're going to have to spend the extra money on the printer and cut corners where we can," she said quickly. "I can tell Takashimaya to use lilies instead of orchids and forget about the peacock feathers around the rims of the vases."

"I can do the invitations," a small, clear voice said from behind them. "For free."

The four girls turned around to see who it was.

Oh look, it's that little Ginny girl, Blair thought. *The ninth grader who did the calligraphy in our school hymnals.*

"I can do them all by hand tonight and put them in the mail. The materials are the only cost, but I know where to get good quality paper cheap," Jenny Humphrey said.

"She did all our hymnals at school," Kati whispered to Tina. "They look really good."

"Yeah," Isabel agreed. "They're pretty cool."

Jenny blushed and stared at the shiny linoleum floor of the coffee shop, waiting for Blair to make up her mind. She knew Blair was the one who mattered.

"And you'll do it all for free?" Blair said, suspiciously.

Jenny raised her eyes. "I was kind of hoping that if I did the invites, maybe I could come to the party?" she said.

Blair weighed the pros and cons in her mind. Pros: The invitations would be unique and best of all, free, so they wouldn't have to skimp on the flowers. Cons: There really weren't any.

Blair looked the Ginny girl up and down. Their cute little ninth-grade helper with the huge chest. She was a total glutton for punishment, and she'd be totally out of place at the party . . . but who cared?

"Sure, you can make yourself an invitation. Make one for one of your friends, too," Blair said, handing the guest list over to Jenny.

How generous.

Blair gave Jenny all the necessary information, and Jenny dashed out of the coffee shop breathlessly. The stores would be closing soon, and she didn't have much time. The guest list was longer than she'd anticipated, and she'd have to stay up all night working on the invitations, but she was going to the party; that was all that mattered.

Just wait until she told Dan. He was going to *freak*. And she was going to make him come with her to the party, whether he liked it or not.

gone with the wind *gone awry*

Two martinis and three rolls of Remi brothers' film later, Serena jumped out of a cab in front of Constance and ran up the stairs to the auditorium, where the interschool play rehearsal had already begun. As always, she was half an hour late.

The sound of a Talking Heads song being played jauntily on the piano drifted down the hallway. Serena pushed open the auditorium door to find her old friend, Ralph Bottoms III, singing *Burning Down the South*, to the tune of *Burning Down the House*, with a completely straight face. He was dressed as Rhett Butler, complete with fake mustache and brass buttons. Ralph had gained weight in the last two years, and his face was ruddy, as if he'd been eating too much rare steak. He was holding hands with a stocky girl with curly brown hair and a heart-shaped face—Scarlett O'Hara. She was singing too, belting out the words in a thick Brooklyn accent.

Serena leaned against the wall to watch, with a mixture of horror and fascination. The scene at the art gallery hadn't fazed her, but this—this was scary.

When the song ended, the rest of the Interschool Drama Club clapped and cheered, and then the drama teacher, an aged English woman, began to direct the next scene.

"Put your hands on your hips, Scarlett," she instructed. "Show me, show me. That's it. Imagine you're the teen sensation of the Civil War South. You're breaking all the rules!"

Serena turned to gaze out the window and saw three girls get out of a cab together on the corner of Ninety-third and Madison. She squinted, recognizing Blair, Kati, and Isabel. Serena hugged herself, warding off the strange feeling that had been stalking her since she'd come back to the city. For the first time in her entire life, she felt left out.

Without a word to anyone in the drama club—*Hello? Goodbye!*—Serena slipped out of the auditorium and into the hallway outside. The wall was littered with flyers and notices and she stopped to read them. One of the flyers was for Vanessa Abrams's film tryout.

Knowing Vanessa, the film was going to be very serious and obscure, but it was better than shouting goofy songs and doing the Hokey-Pokey with fat, red-faced Ralph Bottoms III. Vanessa's tryout had started an hour ago, on a bench in Madison Square Park, but maybe it was still going on. Once again, Serena found herself running for a cab, headed downtown.

"This is how I want you to do it," Vanessa told Marjorie Jaffe, a sophomore at Constance and the only girl who had shown up to try out for the role of Natasha in Vanessa's film. Marjorie had curly red hair and freckles, a little pug nose, and no neck. She chewed gum incessantly, and she was completely, nightmarishly, wrong for the part.

The sun was setting, and Madison Square Park was basked in a pretty pink glow. The air had the distinct smell of New York in autumn, a mixture of smoking fireplaces, dried leaves, steaming hot dogs, dog pee, and bus exhaust.

Daniel was lying on his back on the park bench the way

Vanessa had told him to, a wounded soldier, with his limbs sprawled out pathetically. Wounded in war and in love, he was tragically pale and thin and rumpled-looking. A little glass crack pipe lay on his chest. Lucky Vanessa had found it on the street in Williamsburg that weekend. It was the perfect prop for her sexily damaged prince.

"I'm going to read Natasha's lines. Watch carefully," she told Marjorie. "Okay Dan, let's go."

"Haven't you been asleep?" Vanessa-as-Natasha said, peering at Dan-as-Prince Andrei.

"No, I have been looking at you for a long time. I knew by instinct that you were here. No one except you gives me such a sense of gentle restfulness . . . such light! I feel like weeping from very joy," Dan-as-Prince Andrei said quietly.

Vanessa knelt at his head, her face radiant with solemn delight.

"Natasha, I love you too dearly! More than all the world!" Dan gasped, trying to sit up and then sinking back on the bench as if in pain.

He said he loved her! Vanessa grabbed his hand, her face flushed red at the thrill of it. She was completely caught up in the moment. Then she remembered herself, let go of Dan's hand, and stood up.

"Now your turn," she told Marjorie.

"'Kay," Marjorie said, chewing her gum with her mouth open. She pulled the scrunchy out of her wiry red hair and fluffed it up with her hand. Then she knelt down by Dan's bench and held up the script. "Ready?" she asked him.

Dan nodded.

"Haven't you been asleep?" Marjorie said, batting her eyes flirtatiously and cracking her gum.

Dan closed his eyes and said his line. He could get through this without laughing if he kept his eyes closed.

Halfway through the scene, Marjorie put on a fake Russian accent. It was unbelievably bad.

Vanessa suffered in silence, wondering what she was going to do without a Natasha. For a moment she imagined buying a wig and playing the part herself, getting someone else to shoot it for her. But it was her project; she had to film it.

Just then, someone nudged her arm and whispered, "Do you mind if I try when she's done?"

Vanessa turned to find Serena van der Woodsen standing beside her, a little breathless from running across the park. Her cheeks were flushed and her eyes were as dark as the twilit sky. Serena was her Natasha, if ever there was one.

Daniel bolted upright, forgetting his injuries and his line. The crack pipe rolled to the ground.

"Wait, we're not done," Marjorie said. She prodded Dan in the arm. "You're supposed to kiss my hand."

Dan stared at her blankly.

"Sure," Vanessa told Serena. "Marjorie, do you mind giving Serena your script?"

Serena and Marjorie traded places. Dan had his eyes open now. He didn't dare blink.

They began to read.

"I have been looking at you for a long time," Dan said, meaning every word.

Serena knelt down beside him and took his hand. Dan felt faint, and he was grateful he was lying down.

Whoa. Easy boy.

He had been in lots of plays, but he had never felt that thing called "chemistry" before with anyone. And to be feeling it with Serena van der Woodsen was like dying an exquisite death. It felt like he and Serena were sharing the same breath. He was inhale and she was exhale. He was quiet and still, while she exploded around him like fireworks.

Serena was enjoying herself too. The script was beautiful and passionate, and this scruffy Dan guy was a really good actor.

I could get into this, she thought with a little thrill. She had never really thought about what she wanted to do with her life, but maybe acting was her thing.

They kept reading beyond the given stopping point. It was as though they'd forgotten they were acting. Vanessa frowned. Serena was great—they were great together—but Dan was swooning. It was totally nauseating.

Boys are so predictable, Vanessa thought and cleared her throat noisily. "Thanks, Serena. Thanks, Dan." She pretended to scribble comments in her notebook. "I'll let you know tomorrow, okay?" she told Serena. *In your dreams,* she wrote.

"That was fun!" Serena said, smiling at Dan.

Dan gazed up at her dreamily from the bench, still hungover from the moment.

"Marjorie, I'll let you know tomorrow, too. Okay?" Vanessa told the redhead.

"'Kay," Marjorie said. "Thanks."

Dan sat up, blinking.

"Thanks so much for letting me try out," Serena said sweetly, turning to go.

"See you later," Dan said, sounding drugged.

"Bye," Marjorie said, waving at him, and then rushing after Serena.

"Let's practice your monologue, Dan," Vanessa said sharply. "I want to shoot that first."

"Which subway are you taking?" Marjorie asked Serena, as they walked out of the park.

"Um," Serena said. She never took the subway, but it

wouldn't kill her to ride with Marjorie. "The 6, I guess," she said.

"Hey, me too," Marjorie said happily. "We can ride together."

It was rush hour, and the subway was packed. Serena found herself jammed between a woman with a huge Daffy's bag and a fat little boy with nothing to hold onto but Serena's coat, which he kept grabbing every time the train lurched forward. Marjorie was holding onto the rail above their heads, but only her fingertips could reach it, and she kept staggering backwards, stepping on people's feet.

"Don't you think Dan is majorly cute?" Marjorie asked Serena. "I can't wait until we start filming. I'll get to hang out with him every day!"

Serena smiled. Obviously Marjorie thought she'd gotten the part, which was a little sad, because Serena was absolutely sure that *she* had the part. She had totally nailed it.

Serena imagined getting to know Dan. She wondered which school he went to. He had dark, haunting eyes, and he said his lines like he meant them. She liked that. They'd have to practice quite a bit together after school. She wondered if he liked to go out, and what he liked to drink.

The train came to a sudden stop at Fifty-ninth Street and Lexington—Bloomingdale's. Serena fell forward onto the little boy.

"Ouch," he said, glaring up at her.

"This is my stop," Marjorie said, pushing her way to the door. "Sorry if you didn't get the part. I'll see you at school tomorrow."

"Good luck!" Serena called. The subway car emptied out and she slid into a seat, her mind still on Dan.

She imagined drinking Irish coffees with him in dark cafés and discussing Russian literature. Dan looked like he read a lot. He could give her books to read and help her with her acting. Maybe they'd even become friends. She could use some new ones.

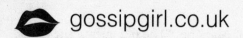

gossipgirl.co.uk

Disclaimer: All the real names of places, people, and events have been altered or abbreviated to protect the innocent. Namely, me.

hey people!

I was in an interschool play once. I had one great line: "Iceberg!" Guess which play I was in and what I was dressed as? The one hundredth person to get it right will win a free Remi brothers poster.

But enough about me.

S'S MODELING DEBUT!

Be on the lookout this weekend for the cool new poster decorating the sides of buses, the insides of subways, the tops of taxis, and available online through yours truly (I'm telling you, I'm connected). It's a great big picture of **S**—not her face, but it has her name on it so you'll know it's her. Congratulations to **S** on her modeling debut!

Sightings

B, *K*, and *I* all in **3 Guys** eating fries and hot chocolates with big fat **Intermix** bags under the table. Don't those girls have anywhere else to go? And we thought they were always out boozing it up and partying down. So disappointing. I did see *B* slip a few splashes of brandy into her hot chocolate, though. Good girl. Also saw that same wigged girl going into the STD clinic downtown. If that is *S*, she's definitely got a bad case of the nasties. Oh, and in case you're wondering why *I* frequent the neighborhood of the STD clinic—I get my hair cut at a very trendy salon across the street.

Your E-mail

 dear gossip girl,
are u really even a girl? u seem like the type 2 pretend to be a girl when u'r really a 50-yrs-old bored journalist with nothing better 2 do than to harsh on kids like me. loser.
—jdwack

A: Dearest Jdwack,

I'm the girliest girl you'd ever want to meet. And I'm pre-college, pre-voting age, too. How do I know *you're* not some fifty-year-old bitter dude with boils on your face taking his inner angst out on innocent girls like me?
—GG

Q: Dear GG,

I loooove your column so much I showed it to my Dad, who totally loved it!! He has friends who work at *Paper* and the *Village Voice* and other magazines. Don't be surprised if your column gets much, much bigger!! I hope you don't mind!!! Love always!!!
—JNYHY

A: *Mind*? No way. I'm all about being big. I'm going to be *huge*. No more crappy one-line parts in interschool plays for me. You might even see *me* on the side of a bus sometime soon.

Bring it *on*!

You know you love me,

gossip girl

dissed at recess

"Yum," Serena said, eyeing the cookies laid out on a table in the Constance lunchroom. Peanut butter cream, chocolate chip, oatmeal. Next to the cookies were plastic cups full of orange juice or milk. A lunch lady was monitoring the cookies, making sure each girl took only two. This was recess, the daily twenty-minute break Constance gave its girls after second period, no matter what grade they were in.

When the lunch lady's head was turned, Serena grabbed six peanut butter creams and glided away to stuff her face. It wasn't exactly a healthy breakfast, but it would have to do. She'd stayed up late the night before trying to read her father's leather-bound edition of *War and Peace* so she'd be better prepared for Vanessa's film.

Whoa, *War and Peace* is like, two million pages long. Ever heard of *CliffsNotes*?

Serena saw Vanessa, wearing her usual black turtleneck and bored expression, coming out of the cafeteria kitchen with a cup of tea in her hand. Serena waved a cookie at her, and Vanessa came over.

"Hi," Serena said cheerfully. "Made up your mind yet?"

Vanessa sipped her tea. She'd been up half the night trying

to decide between Serena and Marjorie for the part. But she couldn't get the look on Dan's face when he read with Serena out of her head. And no matter how good Serena was, she never wanted to see that look on Dan's face again. She certainly didn't want to capture it on film.

"Actually, yes. I haven't told Marjorie yet," Vanessa said calmly, "but I'm giving her the part."

Serena dropped the cookie she was eating on the floor, stunned. "Oh," she said.

"Yeah," said Vanessa, scrambling for a decent reason why she was using Marjorie when Serena was obviously perfect for the part. "Marjorie's really rough and innocent. That's what I'm looking for. Dan and I thought your performance was just a bit too . . . um . . . polished."

"Oh," Serena said again. She could hardly believe it. Even Dan had vetoed her? She had thought they were going to be friends.

"Sorry," Vanessa said, feeling slightly bad. She knew she shouldn't have brought Dan into it; he didn't even know she was turning Serena down. But it sounded more professional that way. Like it wasn't anything she had against Serena personally, not at all. It was strictly a business decision. "You're a good actress though," she added. "Don't be discouraged."

"Thanks," Serena said. Now she wasn't going to hang out with Dan and practice their lines like she'd imagined. And what was she going to tell Ms. Glos? She still didn't have any extracurriculars, and no halfway decent college was going to want her.

Vanessa walked away, looking for Marjorie so she could tell her the good news. She was going to have to change the entire film now that Marjorie was her star. It would have to be a comedy. But at least she had saved herself from making *Endless Love in the Park After Dark*, starring Serena van der Woodsen and Daniel Humphrey. Blech.

Serena stood in the corner of the cafeteria, the remaining cookies crumbling in her hand. *Gone With the Wind* was a total cheese-fest, and she was too polished for *War and Peace*. What else could she do? She chewed on her thumbnail, deep in thought.

Maybe she could make a movie of her own. Blair took film—she could help. When they were younger they'd always talked about making movies. Blair was always going to be the star, wearing cool Givenchy outfits like Audrey Hepburn, except Blair preferred Fendi. And Serena always wanted to direct. She would wear floppy linen pants and shout through a bullhorn and sit in a chair with the word "director" on it.

This was their chance.

"Blair," Serena nearly shouted when she saw Blair by the milk table. She rushed over to her, overcome by the brilliance of her idea. "I need your help," Serena said, squeezing Blair's arm.

Blair kept her body stiff until Serena let go.

"Sorry," Serena said. "Listen, I want to make a movie, and I thought you could help me, you know, with the cameras and stuff, since you take film."

Blair glanced at Kati and Isabel, who were quietly sipping milk behind her. Then she smiled up at Serena, and shook her head. "Sorry, I can't," she said. "I've got activities every single day after school. I don't have time."

"Oh, come on, Blair," Serena said, grabbing Blair's hand. "Remember, we always wanted to do this. You wanted to be Audrey Hepburn."

Blair removed her hand and folded her arms across her chest, glancing at Isabel and Kati again.

"Don't worry, I'll do all the work," Serena added hastily. "All you have to do is show me how to use the camera and the lighting and stuff."

"I can't," Blair insisted. "Sorry."

Serena pursed her lips to keep them from trembling. Her eyes seemed to be growing larger and larger, and her face was turning splotchy.

Blair had seen this transformation in Serena many times as they grew up together. Once, when they were both eight, they had walked the three miles from Serena's country house into the town of Ridgefield to buy ice cream cones. Serena stepped out of the ice cream shop with her triple strawberry cone with chocolate sprinkles and bent down to pet a dog tied up outside. All three scoops fell splat into the dirt. Serena's eyes had grown huge and her face looked like she had the measles. The tears had just started to roll, and Blair was about to offer to share her cone with Serena, when the shop owner came out with a fresh cone for her.

Seeing Serena on the verge of tears once more touched something deep inside of Blair, like an involuntary impulse.

"Um. But we're going out on Friday," she told Serena. "Drinks around eight at the Tribeca Star, if you want to come."

Serena took a deep breath and nodded. "Just like old times," she said, staving off her tears and attempting a smile.

"Right," Blair said.

She made a note in her mental PalmPilot to tell Nate not to come out on Friday now that Serena was coming. Blair's new plan was to knock back a few drinks with Serena at the Tribeca Star, leave early, go home, fill her room with candles, take a bath, and wait for Nate to come. And then they'd have sex all night long to romantic music. She'd already burned a sexy CD to play while they did it.

Even the best-bred girls resort to cheesy things like burning CD mixes when they're losing their virginity.

The bell rang and the girls went their separate ways to class; Blair to her AP Academic-Achievers afternoon, and Serena to her plain old Kraft-American-Slices classes.

Serena couldn't believe she had just been rejected not once but twice in the last ten minutes. And as she gathered her books from her locker, she tried to come up with a new plan of action. She wasn't going to give up.

Her picture wasn't on the side of a bus for nothing.

westsider's romantic dream
up in smoke

Vanessa skipped the first five minutes of Calculus to call Daniel on his cell phone. She knew he had Study Hall fourth period on Thursdays, and he was probably hanging out outside, reading poetry and smoking cigarettes. A girl was using Constance's pay phone in the hallway by the stairs, so Vanessa slipped outside to the pay phone on the corner of Ninety-third Street and Madison.

The lower-school boys were playing dodgeball in the Riverside Prep School courtyard, so when his cell phone rang, Dan was sitting on a park bench in the traffic island in the middle of Broadway. He'd just cracked open *L'Etranger*, by Albert Camus, which he was reading in French class that term. Dan was psyched. He'd already read the English translation, but it felt especially cool to read the French original, especially while sitting outside drinking bad coffee and smoking a cigarette in the middle of noisy, smelly Broadway. It was very hard-core. As people walked past in a hurry to get somewhere, Dan felt aloof and removed from the chaos of everyday life, just like the guy in the book.

Dan had dark circles under his eyes because he hadn't been able to sleep the night before. All he could think about was

Serena van der Woodsen. They were starring in a movie together. They were even going to kiss. It was too good to be true.

Poor dude, he had that right.

His cell phone was still ringing.

"Yeah?" Dan said, answering it.

"Hey. It's Vanessa."

"Hey."

"Listen, I have to make it quick. I just wanted you to know that I told Marjorie she has the part," Vanessa said quickly.

"You mean Serena," Dan said, flicking his ash and taking another puff of his cigarette.

"No, I mean Marjorie."

Dan exhaled and clenched the phone tightly. "Wait. What are you talking about? Marjorie, with the red hair and the gum?"

"Yes, that's right. I haven't got their names mixed up," Vanessa said patiently.

"But Marjorie stank, you can't use her!" Dan insisted.

"Yeah, well, I kind of like that she stank. She's sort of rough around the edges. I think it will make it feel edgier, you know? Like, not what you'd expect," said Vanessa.

"Yeah, definitely not," Dan sneered. "Look, I really think this is a mistake. Serena totally ruled. I don't know why you wouldn't want her. She was awesome."

"Yeah, well, I'm the director, so it's my choice. And I chose Marjorie. Okay?" Vanessa really didn't want to hear about how awesome Serena had been. "Besides, I keep hearing all these stories about Serena. I don't think she's all that reliable."

Vanessa was pretty sure that everything she'd heard was completely bogus, but it couldn't hurt to mention it to Dan.

"What do you mean?" Dan said. "What kind of stories?"

"Like she manufactures her own drug called S, and she has

some pretty bad STDs," Vanessa said. "I really don't want to deal with that."

"Where'd you hear that?" Dan said.

"I have my sources," she said.

A bus roared up Madison on its way to the Cloisters. On the side of it was a massive photograph of a belly button. Or was it a gunshot wound? Scrawled in blue girly writing on the side of the poster was the name "Serena."

Vanessa stared after the bus. Was she losing her mind? Or was Serena really and truly everywhere? Every last bit of her?

"I just don't think she's right for us," Vanessa said, hoping Dan would come around if she used the word "us." It was *their* movie, not hers.

"Fine," Dan said coldly.

"So, are you coming out with me and Ruby in Brooklyn on Friday?" Vanessa asked, eager to change the subject.

"Nah. I don't think so," Dan said. "See ya." He clicked off and tossed the phone angrily into his black courier bag.

That morning his sister Jenny had stumbled into his room, her eyes all bloodshot and her hands covered in black ink, and dropped an invitation to that stupid falcon party on the floor beside his bed. He'd actually dared to think that since he was going to be Serena's costar, he might actually *take* her to the goddamned party. Now, that little dream was all shot to hell.

Dan couldn't believe it. His one chance to get to know Serena was gone because Vanessa wanted to exercise her artistic license to make the worst film ever made. It was unbelievable. More unbelievable still was that Vanessa, queen of the alterna-rebel scene, had actually stooped to spreading rumors about a girl she barely knew. Maybe Constance was finally rubbing off on her.

Oh, don't be a spoilsport. Gossip is sexy. Gossip is good. Not everybody does it, but everybody should!

A bus stopped at a light right in front of him. First Dan noticed Serena's name. It was scrawled in blue, in messy girl's handwriting on a giant black-and-white poster of what looked like a rosebud. It was beautiful.

a fan meets her idol

Jenny was a zombie on Thursday from missing a whole night's sleep, but she'd gotten the *Kiss on the Lips* invitations done, and now she and Dan each had an invitation of their very own.

She was starving, too, having consumed only a banana and an orange for dinner the night before. She'd even skipped her morning chocolate-chip scone. So, at lunch, Jenny wrangled two grilled cheese sandwiches and two coffee yogurts out of the Constance lunch ladies and carried her feast out into the cafeteria, hunting for a seat at a quiet table. While she ate, she had to make up the homework she'd skipped last night.

Jenny chose a table in front of the wall of mirrors on the far side of the cafeteria. None of the older girls liked to eat lunch by the mirrors because it made them feel fat, so that table was always empty. Jenny put her tray down, and was about to start stuffing her face when she noticed a sign-up sheet taped to the mirror.

Jenny lunged for her backpack to find a pen. She scribbled her name at the top of the list—she was the first one to sign up!—and then sat down in front of her heaping tray of food, her heart pounding. Life was full of miracles. It just got better and better.

More miraculous still, Serena van der Woodsen herself was

coming out of the lunch line and making a beeline for Jenny, carrying her tray. Was Serena actually going to sit with her? *In person?*

Deep breath in, deep breath out.

"Hi," Serena said, beaming at Jenny and setting her tray down.

God, she was beautiful. Her hair was the pale gold color some of the other Constance girls tried to achieve by spending four hours in the hair salon on the top floor of Bergdorf Goodman getting their highlights done. But Serena's was natural, you could tell.

"Did I just see you sign up to help with my movie?" Serena asked.

Jenny nodded, speechless in the presence of such greatness.

"Well, you're the only one so far," Serena sighed, sitting down across from Jenny, facing the wall of mirrors. She didn't have to worry about feeling fat when she ate. She didn't have any fat. She raised her golden eyebrows at Jenny. "So, what can you do?"

Jenny poked at her grilled cheese. She couldn't believe she'd gotten two sandwiches. Serena probably thought she was a disgusting pig.

"Well, I'm pretty artistic. I did the school hymnals, you know, in calligraphy? And I've got some photographs in *Rancor* this year, and a short story," Jenny explained.

Rancor was Constance's student-run arts magazine. Vanessa Abrams was the editor.

"Oh, and I just did the invitations for that big party next week that everyone's going to," Jenny said, eager to impress. "Blair Waldorf asked me to do them. Actually . . ." Jenny reached into her bag and pulled out an envelope with Serena's name printed on it in ornate calligraphy. "The guest list Blair gave me still had your boarding school address. I was going to put it in your locker or something," Jenny said, blushing. "But now that you're here . . ." She handed the envelope to Serena.

Do I sound like a stalker? Jenny wondered.

"Thanks," Serena said, taking the envelope. She opened it and read the invitation inside, her eyes dark, her forehead creased in a frown.

Oh, God. She thinks it's ugly! Jenny thought, panicking.

Serena put the invitation in her bag and picked up her fork again, looking distracted. She took a bite of lettuce and chewed on it.

Jenny was taking mental notes on how to act as mysterious, poised, and cool as Serena was acting at that very moment. If only she could have heard the livid thoughts in Serena's head, railing against Blair.

She didn't want me to come to the party. She didn't even tell me there was *a party.*

"Wow," Serena said finally, still munching her lettuce. "Okay, you're hired." She held out her hand and smiled sweetly at Jenny. "I'm Serena," she said.

"I know," Jenny said, blushing even redder. "I'm Jenny."

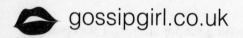
Disclaimer: All the real names of places, people, and events have been altered or abbreviated to protect the innocent. Namely, me.

hey people!

S AND B: HOT IN THE HOT TUB!

This just in from an anonymous source: Apparently, back when they were still tight, **S** and **B** shared a hot hot-tub moment together in **C**'s suite in the **Tribeca Star**. Was the kiss an expression of their true feelings for each other? Or were they just messing around like two silly drunk girls? Either way, it definitely adds a little tension to the mix. What fun!

And in case you haven't seen the poster plastered on all the buses, taxis, and subways all over town, the original photo of **S** can still be seen at the Whitehot Gallery in Chelsea, amidst portraits of other notorious scenesters, myself included. That's right! The Remi brothers were just too sexy to resist. The fabulous are fabulous for a reason, people.

Your E-mail

 Dear Gossip Girl,
I won't tell you who I am, but I'm in the Remi brothers show too. I really love their work, and I love the picture they took of me, but no way would I let them put it on the side of a bus. If you ask me, **S** is asking for whatever she gets. And from what I'm hearing, she's getting it.
—Anonomy

 Dear Anonomy,
It's cool to be modest, but personally, if you wanted to put any bit of me on the side of a bus, I'd be willing. I'm a fame whore.
—GG

Sightings

Little *J* buying a huge book on filmmaking at Shakespeare and Co. on Broadway. *N* hanging out with *C* at a bar over on First Avenue. Guess *N* wants to keep his eye on *C* so *C* doesn't spill the beans, huh? And *B* buying lots of candles in a shop on Lex for her big night with *N*.

That's all for now. Have fun this weekend—I definitely will.

You know you love me,

gossip girl

tribeca star

The Star Lounge in the Tribeca Star Hotel was big and swanky, filled with comfy armchairs and ottomans and circular banquettes, so that the guests could feel like they were having their own private party at each table. One wall was lit with dozens of black candles, flickering in the dimly lit room, and a DJ was playing mellow lounge beats on a turntable. It was only eight o'clock, but the bar was already jammed with people, dressed in the hippest fashions and sipping pastel-colored cocktails.

Blair didn't care what time it was—she needed a drink.

She was sitting in an armchair right near the bar, but the stupid cocktail waitress was ignoring her, probably because Blair hadn't bothered to dress up. She had worn her faded Earl jeans and a boring black sweater because she was only meeting Serena for a quick drink before she went home to prepare for her night of wild sex with Nate. And she wasn't going to dress up for that, either. Blair had decided to meet Nate at the door naked.

Her face grew hot just thinking about it, and she looked around the room self-consciously. She felt like a loser sitting there all by herself without even a drink. Where was Serena, anyway? She didn't have all goddamned night.

Blair lit a cigarette. *If Serena doesn't come by the time I'm done with this cigarette, I'm leaving,* she told herself sulkily.

"Look at *her*," Blair heard a woman say to her friend. "Isn't she beautiful?"

Blair turned to look. Of course it was Serena.

She was wearing blue suede knee-high boots and a real Pucci dress. Long sleeved with a high neck and a crystal beaded belt, in blues, oranges, and greens. It was super fantastic. Her hair was pulled up in a high ponytail on top of her head and she was wearing pale blue eye shadow and creamy pink lipstick. She smiled and waved at Blair from across the room, weaving her way through the crowd. Blair watched the heads turn as she passed, and her stomach churned. She was already sick of Serena, and she hadn't even spoken to her yet.

"Hi," Serena said, plunking herself down on a square ottoman beside Blair's chair.

Immediately, the cocktail waitress appeared.

"Hey Serena, long time no see. How's your brother?" the waitress said.

"Hey Missy. Erik's good. He's too busy to call me ever. I think he must have like, eight different girlfriends up there," Serena laughed. "How are you doing?"

"I'm great," Missy said. "Hey listen, my sister works for a caterer, you know, and she said she saw you a few days ago at a party she was working at a gallery in Chelsea. She said that's you in that picture on all the buses. Is that true?"

"Yeah," Serena said. "Pretty crazy, huh?"

"You are so rad!" Missy squealed. She glanced at Blair who was glaring at her. "Anyway, what can I get you girls?"

"Ketel One and tonic," Blair told her, looking her straight in the eye, daring her to card them. "Extra limes."

But Missy would rather lose her job than hassle Serena van der Woodsen for being underage.

That's the whole reason for going to hotel bars in the first place: no one ever cards.

"And for you, sweetie?" Missy asked Serena.

"Oh, I better start with a Cosmo," Serena said, and laughed. "I need something pink to go with my dress."

Missy hurried away to fetch the drinks, eager to tell the bartender that the girl in the Remi brothers' photo that was all over town was sitting in their bar and they were pals!

"Sorry I'm late," Serena told Blair, looking around. "I thought everyone else would be here with you."

Blair shrugged her shoulders and took a long drag on her dwindling cigarette. "I thought we could hang out by ourselves for a while," she said. "No one really comes out until later, anyway."

"Okay," Serena said. She smoothed out her dress and dug around in her little red purse for her own pack of cigarettes. Gauloises, from France. She tapped one out and stuck it in her mouth. "Want one?" she offered Blair.

Blair shook her head no.

"They're kind of strong, but the box is too cool, I don't care." Serena laughed. She was about to light up with a pack of bar matches, when the bartender swooped in with a lighter.

"Thanks," she said, raising her eyes to look at him. The bartender winked at her and swiftly stepped back behind the bar. Missy brought them their drinks.

"To old times," Serena said, clinking her glass against Blair's and taking a long sip on her pink Cosmopolitan. She sat back on her stool and sighed with pleasure. "Don't you just love hotels?" she said. "They're so full of secrets."

Blair raised her eyebrows at Serena in silent response, sure that Serena was about to tell her all the wild and crazy things that had happened to her in hotels while she was in Europe or wherever, as if Blair cared.

"I mean, don't you always think about what everyone's doing in their rooms? Like, they could be watching pornos and eating cheese doodles, or they could be having kinky sex in the bathroom. Or maybe they're just asleep."

"Uh-huh," said Blair disinterestedly, gulping her drink. She would have to get a little drunk if she were going to make it through the night, especially the naked part. "So what's this about your picture being all over buses and stuff?" Blair said. "I haven't seen it."

Serena giggled and leaned toward Blair confidentially. "Even if you saw it, you probably wouldn't recognize me. It has my name on it, but it's not a picture of my face."

Blair frowned. "I don't get it," she said.

"It's art," Serena said mysteriously, and giggled again. She took a sip of her drink.

The two girls' faces were only inches apart, and Blair could smell the musky essential-oil mixture Serena had started wearing.

"I still don't get it. Is it something dirty?" Blair said, confused.

"Not really," Serena answered with a sly smile. "Lots of people have had theirs done too. You know—celebrities."

"Like who?" Blair said.

"Like Madonna, and Eminem, and Christina Aguilera."

"Oh," Blair said, sounding unimpressed.

Serena's eyes narrowed. "What's that supposed to mean?" she demanded.

Blair lifted her chin and tucked her straight brown hair

behind her ears. "I don't know, it's like you're willing to do anything just to shock people. Don't you have any pride?"

Serena shook her head, still staring at Blair. "Like what? What have I done?" she said, frantically gnawing on her fingernails.

"Like getting kicked out of boarding school," Blair said vaguely.

Serena snorted. "What's so bad about that? Tons of people get kicked out every year. They have so many stupid rules, it's almost impossible *not* to get kicked out."

Blair pressed her lips together, measuring her words carefully. "I don't mean that, I mean *why* you got kicked out." There. She had done it. She had committed herself now. She was going to have to sit and listen to Serena tell her all about the cults she had joined, and the boys she'd had sex with, and the drugs she had done. Shit.

Don't believe for a minute that she wasn't curious, though.

Blair fiddled with the ruby ring on her finger, turning it round and round. Serena raised her glass at Missy, asking for another drink.

"Blair," Serena said. "The only reason I got kicked out was because I didn't show up at the beginning of school. I stayed in France. My parents didn't even know. I was supposed to fly back at the end of August, but I stayed until the third week in September. I was living in this amazing chateau outside of Cannes, and it was like, a constant party. I don't think I slept a whole night the entire time I was there. It was like those parties in that house in *The Great Gatsby*.

"There were these two boys, an older brother and a younger one, and I was totally in love with both of them. Actually," she laughed, "I was even more in love with their father, but he was married."

The Star Lounge DJ switched vibes and began to play a funky acid jazz song with a cool beat. The lights dimmed and the candles flickered. Serena jiggled her foot to the music and glanced at Blair, whose eyes were glazing over.

Serena lit another cigarette and inhaled deeply.

"Anyway, of course I partied a lot at school, but so did everyone else. What the school couldn't deal with was that I didn't even bother to show up at the beginning of the year. I don't blame them, I guess. But to tell you the truth, I really didn't care about going back to school. I was having way too much fun."

Blair rolled her eyes again. She honestly didn't care what the truth was.

"Did you ever think about the fact that these are like, the most important years of our lives? Like, for getting into college and everything?" she said.

Missy brought Serena's drink, and this time Serena only nodded her thanks. She looked down at the floor, her pinky nail between her teeth. "Yeah, I'm just realizing that now," she admitted. "I hadn't thought about it before—how I should have been joining teams and clubs. You know, getting really into the school thing."

Blair shook her head. "I feel sorry for your parents," she said quietly.

Serena's eyes were getting big, and her lip was trembling. But she was determined not to let Blair make her cry. Blair was just being a bitch, that's all. Maybe she was getting her period.

Serena took a huge gulp of her drink and wiped her mouth with her cocktail napkin. "So, you never told me what you and Nate did all summer. Did you ever go up to Maine and see that boat he built?" she asked, completely changing the subject.

Blair shook her head. "I had tennis camp. It sucked."

"Oh," Serena said.

They drank their drinks in awkward silence.

Serena sat up suddenly, remembering something. "Hey," she said. "You know, some girl actually signed up to help me with my movie? A ninth grader. Her name is Jenny. And she gave me an invitation to that party next week. You know, the one you've been planning?"

Touché, girlfriend. *Touché*.

Blair pulled another cigarette out of the pack and stuck it in her mouth. She reached for a match, pausing before she struck it to see if the bartender would leap across the room with a lighter. He didn't. Blair lit the cigarette herself and blew a big cloud of smoke directly into Serena's face.

So Serena knew about the party. She had an invitation. Well, she was bound to find out anyway.

"The calligrapher," Blair said, smiling sweetly. "She's good, isn't she?"

"Yeah, she did a great job," Serena said. "And it was really nice of her to notice that mine had the wrong address on it. She said the address you gave her was my dorm room at Hanover."

Blair tucked her hair behind her ears and shrugged her shoulders. "Oops," she said, feigning cluelessness. "Sorry about that."

"So tell me about the party," Serena said. "What's it for again?"

Blair couldn't talk about the cause without smiling self-consciously because it sounded so lame and unsexy. That's why she'd named the party *Kiss on the Lips*. To give it some allure. "It's for those two peregrine falcons that live in Central Park. They're an endangered species, and everyone's worried that they're going to die or starve or the squirrels will raid their nests or whatever. So they set up a foundation for them," she explained. "Don't laugh. I know it's kind of stupid."

Serena blew out a puff of smoke and giggled. "Well, it's not like there aren't *people* that need saving. I mean, what about the homeless?"

"Well, it's as good a cause as any. We wanted something that wasn't too heavy to start the season off," Blair huffed, annoyed. It was fine for *her* to laugh at the cause she'd chosen for the party, but Serena had no right.

Serena steered the conversation back on course. "So is the party like, just for us, or is it for parents, too?" she asked.

Blair hesitated. "Just . . . us," she said finally. She downed the rest of her drink and looked at her watch. "Um, I kind of have to take off," she said. She slid her bag over her arm and picked her pack of cigarettes up off the table.

Serena frowned. She had taken her time getting dressed, psyching herself up for a wild night out with her friends. She'd expected a big group—Blair and the other girls, Nate and his gang, Chuck and his boys—all the people they always used to hang out with.

"But I thought we would stay here for a while. Wait for everyone else," Serena said. "Where are you going, anyway?"

"I have a practice SAT tomorrow morning," Blair said, feeling extremely superior, even though she was lying her ass off. "I need to prepare for it, and I want to go to bed early."

"Oh," Serena said. She crossed her arms and sat back on her stool. "I was hoping we'd all wind up partying in the Basses' suite upstairs. They still have it, don't they?"

Back in tenth grade, Serena and Blair and her friends had spent many a night in Chuck Bass's suite, drinking and dancing, watching movies and ordering room service, taking hot tubs. Together, they'd pass out on the king-sized bed and stay there until they were sober enough to make their way home.

Once, during a very drunken night at the end of tenth grade, Serena and Blair were soaking in the hot tub, and Blair had kissed Serena full on the lips. Serena hadn't seemed to remember it the next morning, but Blair never forgot it. Even though it was just an impulse move that didn't mean anything, thinking about that kiss always made her feel hot and itchy and uncomfortable. That was another reason why it had been such a relief when Serena went away.

"The Basses still have the suite," Blair said, standing up. "But they really don't appreciate people using it. This isn't tenth grade anymore," she added coldly.

"Okay," Serena said. She couldn't say anything right, could she? At least, not to Blair.

"Well, have a good weekend," Blair said with a stiff smile, as if they'd only just met. As if they hadn't known each other all their lives. She dropped twenty dollars on the table for their drinks. "Excuse me," she told the three tall boys who were blocking her path. "Can I get by?"

Serena twirled her drink straw around in her glass and sipped the dregs of her Cosmopolitan, watching Blair leave. The drink tasted salty now, because she was about to cry again.

"Hey Blair—" Serena called out after her friend. Maybe if she just blurted it all out, asked Blair why she was really mad, even confessed to sleeping with Nate that one time, they could go on being friends. They could start over. Serena might even start taking an SAT prep course, so they could take practice SATs together, or whatever.

But Blair kept on pushing her way through the crowd and out the door to the street.

She walked over to Sixth Avenue to catch a cab back

uptown. It was starting to rain and her hair was frizzing. A bus roared by with Serena's picture on the side of it. Was it her belly button? It looked like the dark pit at the center of a peach. Blair turned her back on it and waved her hand in the air to flag down the next taxi. She couldn't get away fast enough. But the first taxi that stopped for her had the same poster in the lighted advertising box on its roof. Blair got in and slammed the door angrily. She could never get completely away—Serena was fucking everywhere.

b & n come close, but no cigar

Serena reached for another cigarette and stuck it in her mouth with trembling fingers. Suddenly a pinky-ringed hand proffered a Zippo and lit the cigarette for her. The lighter was gold, with the monogram *C.B.* So was the ring.

"Hey Serena. You look seriously hot," Chuck Bass said. "What are you doing sitting here all by yourself?"

Serena inhaled deeply, quelling her tears, and smiled. "Hey Chuck. I'm glad you're here. Blair ditched me and now I'm all alone. Is anyone else coming?"

Chuck clicked his lighter shut and put it in his pocket. He glanced around the room. "Who knows?" he said casually. "They could come, or they could not come." He sat down in the armchair where Blair had been sitting. "You really do look hot," he said again, staring at Serena's legs like he wanted to eat them.

"Thanks," Serena said and laughed. It was kind of a relief to see that Chuck was still exactly the same, even if everyone else was acting like freaks. She had to love him for that.

"Another round," Chuck called over to Missy. "And put everything on my tab." He handed Serena the twenty Blair had left on the table. "You can keep that," he said.

"But it's Blair's," Serena said, taking the bill and looking at it.

"Give it back to her, then," Chuck said.

Serena nodded and stuffed the bill into her red velvet handbag.

"There you go," Chuck said, when Missy put the drinks down. "Bottoms up!" He clinked glasses with Serena and poured scotch down his throat.

"Oops," she said, as her Cosmo sloshed onto her dress. "Damn."

Chuck grabbed his cocktail napkin and dabbed at the stain, which happened to be on her hip. "There, you can't even see it," he said, letting his hand linger near her crotch.

Serena grabbed Chuck's hand and put it back in his lap. "Thanks, Chuck," she said. "I think I'm okay."

Chuck wasn't even a tad embarrassed. He was unembarrassable.

"Hey, let's get one more drink and take it up to my suite, okay?" he offered. "I'll tell the bar staff to tell anyone who comes to meet us up there. They know who my friends are."

Serena hesitated, thinking about what Blair had said about the Basses not liking people in their suite anymore. "Are you sure it's okay?" she said.

Chuck laughed and stood up, holding out his hand to her. "Of course it's okay. Come on."

Even though it was raining out and he was freezing his ass off, Nate was in no hurry to get to Blair's house. It was pretty ironic, really. Here he was, a seventeen-year-old guy, about to have sex with his girlfriend for the first time (hers, anyway). He should have been *running*.

She must know by now, he kept telling himself, over and over and over. How could she not? The whole city had to know by now that he had had sex with Serena. But if Blair knew, then why hadn't she said anything?

Thinking about it was driving Nate insane.

He ducked into a liquor store on Madison Avenue and bought a half pint of Jack Daniels. He'd already smoked a little joint at home, but he'd need a shot of courage before he saw Blair. He had no idea what he was in for.

Nate walked the rest of the way as slowly as he could, taking surreptitious sips from the bottle. Just before turning down Seventy-second Street to her apartment, he bought Blair a rose.

Chuck ordered another round of drinks from the bar, and Serena followed him into the elevator and up to the Basses' ninth-floor suite. It looked exactly the same as it always had: living room with entertainment center and bar; huge bedroom with king-sized bed and another entertainment center, as if they needed two; huge marble bathroom with hot tub and two fluffy white bathrobes. That was other great thing Serena loved about hotels—the bathrobes.

Doesn't everyone?

On the coffee table in the living room was a pile of photographs. Serena recognized Nate's face in the top one and she picked them up and shuffled through them.

Chuck glanced at the pictures over her shoulder. "Last year," he said, shaking his head. "We were pretty crazy."

Blair, Nate, Chuck, Isabel, Kati, everyone was in them, naked in the hot tub, dancing in their underwear, drinking champagne in bed. They were all party shots from last year—the date was in the corner of each one—and they were all taken in the suite.

So Blair had lied. Everyone did still party in the Basses' suite, same as always. And Blair wasn't the little goody-goody she pretended to be either with her mock SAT and her prim black cardigan. In one picture Blair was wearing only her underwear, jumping up and down on the bed with a magnum of champagne in her hand.

Serena gulped her drink and sat down on one end of the couch. Chuck sat down at the other end and pulled her feet into his lap.

"Chuck," Serena warned.

"What? I'm taking your boots off for you," Chuck said innocently. "Don't you want to take them off?"

Serena sighed. She felt tired all of a sudden, really tired. "Yeah, sure," she said. She reached for the remote and clicked on the television while Chuck removed her boots. *Dirty Dancing* was on TBS. Perfect.

Chuck began to massage her feet. It felt good. He bit her big toe and kissed her ankle.

"Chuck," Serena giggled, falling back on the couch and closing her eyes. The room tilted a bit. She never could hold her liquor.

Chuck worked his hands up her legs. Within seconds his fingers were plying the insides of her thighs.

"Chuck," Serena said, opening her eyes again and sitting up. "Do you mind if we just sit here? We don't have to do anything, okay? Let's just hang out on the couch and watch *Dirty Dancing*. You know, like girls."

Chuck crawled towards Serena on his hands and knees until he was looming over her and she was pinned beneath him. "But I'm not a girl," he said. He lowered his face to hers, and began to kiss her. His mouth tasted like peanuts.

"Shit!" Blair shrieked when she heard the doorman buzz from downstairs. She was still wearing her clothes, and she had just spilled red candle-wax all over her rug.

Blair switched off her bedroom light and ran to answer the buzzer in the kitchen.

"Yes, send him up," she told the doorman. She unbuttoned her jeans and flew back to her room, wriggling out of them. Then she pulled the rest of her clothes off and tossed them into the closet. Naked, she spritzed herself with her favorite perfume, even spritzing once between her legs.

Oooh, *bad girl.*

Blair checked out her naked body in the mirror. Her legs were too short for the rest of her body, and her boobs were small and not as "pay attention to me" as she would have liked them. Her jeans had left an angry red mark on her waist, but it was barely noticeable in the dim candlelight. Her skin was still nice and tan from the summer, but her face seemed young and scared, not nearly as sexy as it was supposed to look. And her hair was sticking up in a halo of frizz from the rain. Blair dashed into the bathroom and applied a coat of the lip gloss Serena had left on her sink to her lips and ran her hairbrush through her long brown hair until it cascaded onto her shoulders in the sexiest way possible. There, instant irresistibility.

The doorbell rang. Blair dropped her hairbrush, and it clattered into the sink.

"Hold on!" she called out. She took a deep breath and closed her eyes to say a little prayer, although she wasn't exactly the praying type.

I hope it goes well. It was the best she could do.

Serena let Chuck kiss her for a while because he was heavy and she couldn't get him off her. As he explored the inside of her mouth with his tongue, she watched Jennifer Grey splash around in a lake with Patrick Swayze. Finally, Serena turned her head away and closed her eyes.

"Chuck, I really don't feel so well," she said, pretending she was about to be sick. "Do mind if I just lie here for a little while?"

Chuck sat up and wiped his mouth with the back of his hand. "Sure, that's cool," he said. He stood up. "I'll go get you some water."

Chuck went over to the wet bar and filled up a glass with ice, pouring in a bottle of Poland Spring water.

When he turned to take the water back to Serena, she was already asleep. Her head had fallen back against the cushions, and her long legs twitched. Chuck sank onto the couch beside her, grabbed the clicker, and changed the channel.

"Hi," Blair said, opening the door a crack and poking her face through it.

"Hi," Nate said, holding the rose. His hair was wet and his cheeks were pink.

"I'm naked," Blair told him.

"Really?" Nate said, barely absorbing the information. "Can I come in?"

"Sure," Blair said, opening the door wide.

Nate stared at her, frozen in the doorway.

Blair blushed, hugging her arms around herself. "I told you I was naked." She reached her hand out to take the flower.

Nate pressed it into her hand. "I got that for you," he said gruffly. Then he cleared his throat and looked at the floor. "Should I take off my shoes?"

Blair laughed and opened the door wider. Nate was nervous, even more nervous than she was. He was so sweet.

"Just hurry up and take your clothes off," she said. She took his hand. "It's okay. Come on."

Nate followed her into her bedroom, not doing any of the things a boy should normally have done under the circumstances. Like check out Blair's bare ass, or worry about condoms, or bad breath, or try to say the right thing. He was barely thinking at all.

Blair's room was a blaze of candles. A bottle of red wine was open on the floor, with two glasses beside it. Blair knelt down and poured each of them a glass like a little geisha. She felt more comfortable naked in the darkness of her room.

"What kind of music do you want to listen to?" she asked Nate, handing him a glass.

Nate gulped the wine, swallowing noisily. "Music? Anything you want. Whatever," he said.

Of course, Blair had her CD mix all cued up. The first song was Coldplay, because she knew Nate liked them.

Slow and sexy, rocker boy.

Blair had made and remade the movie of this moment in her head so many times she felt like an actress who was finally getting her big break, playing the role of her career.

She reached up and put her hands on Nate's shoulders. He tried not to look at her, but he couldn't help it. She was naked, and she was beautiful. She was a girl and he was a boy.

There have been plenty of songs written about this.

"Take off your clothes, Nate," Blair whispered.

Maybe after we do it, I'll tell her, Nate thought.

That didn't seem completely fair, but still, he kissed her. And once he started, he couldn't stop.

When Serena woke up a little while later, Chuck had changed the channel to MTV2 and was singing along loudly to Jay-Z. Serena's Pucci dress had ridden up above her waist, and her lacy blue underwear was showing.

Serena propped herself up on her elbows and wiped the lipgloss scum out of the corners of her mouth. She pulled down her dress. "What time is it?" she said.

Chuck glanced at her. "Time for us to take off our clothes and get in bed," he said impatiently. He'd been waiting long enough.

Serena's head felt thick, and she was dying for a glass of water. "I feel awful," she said, sitting up and rubbing her forehead. "I want to go home."

"Come on," Chuck said, flicking off the TV. "We could take a hot tub first. That'll make you feel better."

"No," Serena insisted.

"Fine," Chuck said angrily. He stood up. "There's water on the table. Put your boots on, I'll help you get a cab."

Serena pulled on her boots and stared at the cold rain falling outside the hotel room window.

"It's raining," she said, taking a sip of the water.

Chuck handed her a scarf, his trademark blue cashmere, monogrammed with the letters *C.B.* "Wrap it around your head," he said. "Come on, let's go."

Serena took the scarf and followed Chuck out to the elevator. They rode down in silence. Serena knew Chuck was disappointed that she was leaving, but she didn't care. She couldn't wait to get out into the fresh air and into her own bed.

A cab pulled up, the Remi brothers' poster in the box on the cab's roof. Serena thought it looked like a close-up photograph of lips puckered into a kiss.

"What's that? Mars?" Chuck joked, pointing to it. He glanced at Serena without a trace of humor in his eyes. "No, it's your anus!"

Serena blinked at him. She couldn't tell if Chuck trying to be funny or if that's what he actually thought the picture was.

Chuck held the cab door open for her, and she slid into the back seat.

"Thanks, Chuck," she said sweetly, "I'll see you soon, okay?"

"Whatever," Chuck said. He leaned into the cab and pressed Serena against the seat. "What's your problem anyway?" he hissed. "You've been fucking Nate Archibald since tenth grade, and I'm sure you did just about every guy at boarding school, and in France, too. What, are you like, too good to give me some?"

Serena stared directly into Chuck's eyes, seeing him as he really was for the first time. He'd always been hard to like, but she'd never actually hated him before.

"That's okay, I wouldn't want to do it with you anyway," Chuck sneered. "I hear you have diseases."

"Get away from me," Serena hissed, putting her hands on his chest and shoving him away. She slammed the cab door shut in his face, and gave the driver her address.

As the cab pulled away, Serena hugged herself, staring straight ahead through the rain-spattered windshield. When the taxi stopped at a light on the corner of Broadway and Spring, she opened the door, leaned out, and threw up into the gutter.

That will teach her not to drink on an empty stomach.

Chuck's scarf swung from her neck and dangled in the puddle of pink vomit on the pavement. Serena pulled the scarf off, wiped her mouth on it, and stuffed it into her bag.

"Gross," she said, slamming the cab door closed again.

"Tissue, miss?" the cab driver offered, passing a box of Kleenex back to her.

Serena pulled one from the box and wiped her mouth with it. "Thanks," she said.

Then she sat back in the seat and closed her eyes, grateful, as always, for the kindness of strangers.

"What about a condom or something?" Blair murmured, gaping at Nate's hard-on. It looked like it was going to take over the world.

She had managed to get all of his clothes off, and now they were lying down on her bed on top of the covers. They'd been fooling around for almost an hour. On the stereo, the Jennifer Lopez song "Love Don't Cost a Thing" was playing, and Blair was getting hotter and hotter. She reached for Nate's hand and licked his fingers, sucking greedily on the tip of each one. She had a feeling sex was going to be even better than food.

Nate rolled onto his back while Blair sucked his fingers. He had been so uptight about seeing Blair that he hadn't eaten dinner, and now he was feeling hungry. Maybe when he went home he'd pick up a burrito from the Mexican place on Lexington Avenue. That's what he wanted, a chicken and black bean burrito with extra guacamole.

Blair bit down hard on his pinky.

"Ow," Nate said, his hard-on deflating as if it had been pricked with a pin. He sat up and ran his hands through his hair. "I can't do this," he muttered under his breath.

"What?" Blair said, sitting up too. "What's wrong?" Her heart fell. This wasn't in the script. Nate was ruining a perfect moment.

Clumsily, Nate took Blair's hand and looked into her eyes for the first time all night. "I have to tell you something," he said. "I can't do this without you knowing. I feel like an asshole."

Blair could tell by the look in Nate's eyes that the moment wasn't just ruined, it was killed. "What?" she said softly.

Nate reached down and gathered up the edges of the quilt. He draped one end around Blair's shoulders and wrapped the other end around his waist. It didn't seem right to talk about this when they were both so naked. He took Blair's hand again.

"Remember the summer before last when you were away in Scotland, at your aunt's wedding?" Nate began.

Blair nodded.

"It was so friggin' hot that summer. I was in the city with my Dad, just hanging out while he went to some meetings and stuff. I got bored, so I called Serena in Ridgefield, and she came down." Nate noticed Blair's back stiffen when he mentioned Serena's name. She removed her hand from his and crossed her arms over her chest, her eyes suddenly distrustful.

"We had some drinks and sat out in the garden. It was so hot, Serena started splashing around in the fountain, and then she started splashing me. And I guess I got kind of carried away. I mean—" Nate fumbled. He remembered what Cyrus had told him about girls liking surprises. Well, Blair was about to be very surprised, and he didn't think she was going to like it one bit.

"And what?" Blair demanded. "What happened?"

"We kissed," Nate said. He took a deep breath and held it. He couldn't just leave it at that. He blew the breath out. "And then we had sex."

Blair threw the quilt off her shoulders and stood up. "I knew it!" she shouted. "Who *hasn't* had sex with Serena? That nasty, slutty *bitch*!"

"I'm sorry, Blair. But it wasn't like, planned or anything," Nate said. "It just happened. And it was only that one time, promise. I just didn't want you to think this was my first time, when it wasn't. I had to tell you."

Blair stomped into her bathroom and snatched her pink satin bathrobe off its hook. She put it on, cinching the belt tight. "Get the fuck out of here, Nate," she said, angry tears sluicing her cheeks. "I can't even look at you. You're pathetic."

"Blair—" Nate pleaded. For a split second he tried to think of something charming to say. He could usually think of something, but nothing came.

Blair slammed the bathroom door shut in his face.

Nate stood up and pulled on his boxers. Kitty Minky poked her head out from under the bed and stared at him accusingly, her golden cat eyes glowing eerily in the dark. Nate grabbed his jeans, shirt, and shoes and headed for the front door. He could hardly wait for that burrito.

The front door closed with a hollow bang, but Blair remained locked in the bathroom, standing in front of the mirror glaring at her tear-stained reflection. The tube of Serena's lip gloss was still lying on the sink where she had left it. Blair picked it up with trembling fingers. *Gash*, it was called. What an ugly name. Of course Serena could wear lip gloss with ugly names, and tights with holes in them, and dirty old shoes, and never cut her hair, and still get the boy. Blair grunted at the irony of it all and opened her bathroom window, tossing the lip gloss out into the night and waiting to hear it land on the pavement below. But she couldn't hear a thing.

Her head was too full of the new movie she was working on. The movie in which the fabulous Serena van der Woodsen was run over by a bus with her stupid picture plastered to the side of it and was horribly maimed. Her old friend Blair would take time out from her busy life with her doting husband, Nate, to feed Elephant Girl Serena mashed pears and tell her all about the parties she and Nate had been to. Serena would grunt and fart in response, but charitable Blair wouldn't mind. It was the least she could do. Everyone would call her *Saint Blair*, and she would win awards for her golden heart.

will *s* & *n* hook up again?

Just before midnight, the taxi pulled up at 994 Fifth Avenue. Across the street, the steps of the Metropolitan Museum of Art were deserted, glowing eerily white in the light of the street-lamps. Serena stepped out of the cab and waved to Roland, the old night doorman, who was dozing just inside the lobby. The door to the apartment building opened, but it wasn't Roland who opened it. It was Nate.

"Nate!" Serena squealed, genuinely surprised. "Hey, could you loan me five bucks? I haven't got enough cash. Usually the doorman helps me out, but I guess he's asleep."

Nate pulled a wad of bills out of his pocket and gave some to the taxi driver. He put his finger to his lips and crept up to the front door of the building. Then he knocked loudly on the glass door. "Hello?" he shouted.

"Oh, Nate," Serena laughed. "You are so mean!"

Roland snapped his eyes open and nearly fell off his chair. Then he opened the door for them, and Serena and Nate ran inside and rode the elevator up to Serena's apartment.

Serena led the way to her room and sat down heavily on the bed. "Did you get my message?" she yawned at Nate, pulling off her boots. "I thought you'd come out tonight."

"I couldn't," Nate said. He picked up the little glass ballerina perched on top of Serena's mahogany jewelry chest. She had the tiniest toes, like little pinpoints. He'd forgotten about her.

"Well, it wasn't worth it anyway," Serena sighed. She lay down on the bed. "I am so tired," she said. She patted the bed next to her and slid over to give Nate room. "Come lie down and tell me a bedtime story?"

Nate put the ballerina down and swallowed. Breathing in the scent of Serena's room with Serena in it made his heart hurt. He lay down next to her, their bodies touching. Nate put his arm around Serena and she kissed his cheek, snuggling in close.

"I was just over at Blair's," Nate said.

But Serena didn't answer. She was breathing steadily. Maybe she was already asleep.

Nate lay still, with his eyes open wide, his mind racing. He wondered if he and Blair were officially broken up now. He wondered if he kissed Serena right now, full on the lips and told her he loved her, how she'd respond. He wondered if he'd just gone ahead and had sex with Blair if everything would have been all right.

Nate cast his eyes around the room, taking in all the familiar well-loved objects that he'd grown up seeing and forgotten all about. The kilt-wearing teddy bear from Scotland that sat aristocratically on Serena's little dressing table. The big mahogany armoire with its drawers half open and all her clothes spilling out of it. The little brown burn mark he'd made in ninth grade on the white canopy hanging from her bed.

On the floor by the door was Serena's red velvet bag. The contents had spilled out of it. A blue pack of Gauloise cigarettes. A twenty-dollar bill. An Amex card. And a navy blue scarf with the letters *C.B.* stitched on it in gold.

Why had she needed to borrow money from him when she

had twenty dollars with her? Nate wondered. And what the hell was she doing with Chuck Bass's scarf?

Nate turned over on his side and Serena moaned softly as her head rolled back on the pillow. He studied her critically. She was so beautiful and sexy and trusting, and so full of surprises. It was hard to believe she was actually for real.

Serena reached up and put her arms around Nate's neck, pulling him toward her.

"Come on," she murmured, her eyes still closed. "Sleep with me."

Nate's whole body tensed. He didn't know if Serena meant just go to sleep or *sleep with her*, but he was definitely aroused. Any boy in his right mind would be, which is exactly what turned Nate off.

There was something so careless about the way Serena had said it. Nate suddenly had no trouble imagining her doing the things he'd heard she'd done. With Serena, anything was possible.

A glitter of silver caught his eye. It was the tiny silver box Serena kept on her bedside table, full of her baby teeth. Every time he came over, Nate used to open up the velvet-lined box to see if all the teeth were still there. But not this time. From the look of things, Serena wasn't the same little girl who'd lost all those teeth.

Nate pulled away from her and stood up. He snatched up Chuck's scarf and tossed it on the bed, not noticing that it was streaked with vomit. And then, without even looking at Serena again, he left, slamming the door behind him.

Chicken.

At the sound of the door closing Serena opened her eyes and breathed in the scent of her own barf. Gagging, she threw the covers back and ran to the bathroom. She clutched the rim of her white porcelain sink and heaved into it, her sides hurting with the effort. Nothing came out. Serena turned on the shower as hot as it would go and pulled her clammy Pucci dress over her head, dropping it on the floor. All she needed was a good hot shower and a little exfoliant.

Tomorrow she'd be good as new.

Disclaimer: All the real names of places, people, and events have been altered or abbreviated to protect the innocent. Namely, me.

hey people!

THE VIRGIN ISSUE

Can you believe **N**? He was *thisclose* to getting a nice slice of **B** pie, if you know what I mean. I guess we're supposed to admire his self-control, his ability to keep the old hot dog in the bun. But I bet **B** really wouldn't have minded too much if **N** had just kept his mouth shut and got on with it instead of getting all moral on her and telling her all about his time with **S**. I mean, who's **B** going to lose it to now?

I was wrong about boys. I always thought they'd do anything to bag a virgin. I mean, I thought **N** would *like* the idea that **B** has never done it. But he doesn't seem to care about that at all. All it does is make having sex with her this huge thing that he can't deal with without smoking a big fattie and downing half a bottle of JD. So disappointing.

Not that he was too quick to jump **S**'s bones either, and we all know she's no virgin.

Maybe **N** just has high moral standards.

Ooh, that makes me like him even more.

Your E-mail

Hey gossip girl,
i saw **S** go upstairs with some dude at the Tribeca Star. she was wasted. i was kind of tempted to knock on the door and see if there was a party going on or s/t, but i chickened out. i just wanted your advice. do you think she'd do me? i mean, she looks pretty easy.
—Coop

Dear Coop,
If you're the type of guy who has to ask, then probably not.
S may be a ho, but she has excellent taste.
—GG

Sightings

Just one: **N** at the burrito place on Lexington, chatting up the cute girl behind the counter. She gave him extra guacamole for free. Yeah, I bet she did.

You know you love me,

gossip girl

westsiders go bonkers for barneys

"Dan," Jenny whispered, poking at her brother's chest. "Wake up."

Dan flung his hand over his eyes and kicked at his sheets. "Go away. It's Saturday," he mumbled.

"Please get up," Jenny whined. She sat down on the bed, poking him repeatedly until he removed his arm to glare at her.

"What's your problem?" Dan said. "Leave me alone."

"No," Jenny insisted. "We have to go shopping."

"Right," Dan said. He rolled over, turning his head toward the wall.

"Please, Dan. I have to get a dress for the party on Friday and you have to help me. Dad gave me his credit card. He said you could get a tux, too." Jenny giggled. "Since we're turning out to be the type of spoiled rotten kids that will need tuxes and dresses and all that crap."

Dan rolled over. "I'm not going to that party," he said.

"Shut up. Yes you are. You're going and you're going to meet Serena and dance with her. I'll introduce you. She's totally cool," Jenny burbled happily.

"No," Dan said stubbornly.

"Well, you can at least help me pick out a dress," Jenny pouted. "Because I'm going. And I want to look nice."

"Can't Dad go with you?" Dan asked.

"Yeah, right. I said I wanted to look nice," Jenny scoffed. "You know what Dad told me? He said, 'Go to Sears, it's the *proletarian* department store.' Whatever that means. I don't even know where Sears *is*, if it even exists anymore. Anyway, I want to go to Barneys. I can't believe I've never even been there. I bet people like Serena van der Woodsen and Blair Waldorf go there, like, every day."

Dan sat up and yawned loudly. Jenny was all dressed and ready to go, with her curly hair pulled back into a ponytail. She even had her jacket and shoes on. She looked so cute and eager, it was kind of hard to say no.

"You're such a pain in my ass," Dan said, standing up and stumbling toward the bathroom.

"You know you love me," Jenny called after him.

As far as Dan was concerned, Barneys was full of assholes, down to the dude who opened the door for him, smiling in the cheesiest way possible. But Jenny loved it, and even though she had never been there, she seemed to know everything about the place. She knew not to bother with the lower floors, which were full of designer clothes she could never afford, and headed straight to the top floor Co-op. And when the elevator doors rolled open, she felt like she had died and gone to heaven. There were so many beautiful dresses hanging on the racks it made her salivate to look at them. She wanted to try them all on, but of course she couldn't.

When you're a 34D, you're kind of limited. And you definitely need *help*.

"Dan, will you go ask that woman to help me find this in my size," Jenny whispered, fingering a purple velvet empire-waist sheath with beaded straps. She pulled out the price tag. Six hundred bucks.

"Jesus Christ!" Dan said, looking at the price over her shoulder. "No way."

"I'm just trying it on for fun," Jenny insisted. "I won't buy it." She held the dress up to herself. The bodice would barely cover her nipples. Jenny sighed and put the dress back on the rack. "Would you please ask that lady if she'll help me?" she repeated.

"Why can't you ask?" Dan said. He shoved his hands in his corduroys and leaned against a wooden hat rack.

"Please?" Jenny said.

"Fine."

Dan strode over to a haggard looking woman with frosted blond hair. She looked like she'd been working in department stores her entire life, only taking one vacation a year in Atlantic City, New Jersey. Dan imagined her chain-smoking Virginia Slims down on the boardwalk, worrying about how the girls back at the store were managing without her.

"Can I help you, young man?" the woman asked him. Her name tag said "Maureen."

Dan smiled. "Hello. Do you think you could help my sister find a nice dress? She's over there." He pointed at Jenny, who was studying the price tag of a red silk wraparound with ruffles on the sleeves. Jenny had taken off her jacket and was wearing a white T-shirt. Dan could not deny it. Her boobs were really huge.

"Yes, of course," Maureen said, striding purposefully toward Jenny.

Dan stayed where he was, glancing around the room and feeling completely out of place. Behind him, he heard a familiar voice.

"I look like a nun, Mom, I swear. It's just completely wrong."

"Oh, Serena," another voice said. "I think it's darling. What if you just unbutton the collar a bit. There. See? It's very Jackie O."

Dan spun around. A tall, middle-aged woman with Serena's coloring was standing half in, half out of a curtained dressing room. The curtain was slightly parted, and Dan could just see a bit of Serena's hair, her collarbone, her bare feet, the toenails painted dark red. His cheeks burned, and he bolted for the elevator.

"Hey Dan, where're you going?" Jenny called over to him. Her arms were already piled high with dresses, and Maureen was flicking efficiently through the racks, while giving her all sorts of good advice about support bras and the latest figure-enhancing underwear. Jenny had never been happier.

"Gonna check out the men's stuff," Dan mumbled, glancing nervously toward the side of the room where he'd spotted Serena.

"Okay," Jenny said gaily. "I'll meet you down there in forty-five minutes. And if I need your help, I'll call you on your cell."

Dan nodded and leapt onto the elevator as soon as it opened. Down in the men's department, he ambled over to a counter and spritzed his hands with Gucci cologne, wrinkling his nose at the strong, Italian, male scent. He looked around the intimidating, woody room for a bathroom where he could wash it off. Instead, he found a mannequin in full evening dress and beside it, a rack full of tuxes. Dan fingered the rich material of the jackets and looked at the labels. Hugo Boss, Calvin Klein, DKNY, Armani.

He imagined stepping out of a limo wearing his Armani tux with Serena on his arm. They'd stroll down the red carpet leading into the party, music thumping all around them, and people would turn and say, "Oh," in hushed voices. Serena would press her perfect mouth to Dan's ear. "I love you," she'd whisper. Then Dan would stop and kiss her and pick her up and carry her back to the limo. Screw the party. They had better things to do.

"Can I help you, sir?" A salesman asked.

Dan turned abruptly. "No. I—" He hesitated and looked at his watch. Jenny was going to take forever upstairs, and why shouldn't he? As long as he was there. He picked up the Armani tux and held it out to the sales guy. "Can I try this one on in my size?" he said.

The cologne must have gone to his head.

Jenny and Maureen had completely scoured the racks, and Maureen had filled a dressing room with dozens of possibilities in assorted sizes. The problem with Jenny was she was only a size two, but her chest was a size eight at least. Maureen thought they'd have to compromise and go for a six, letting it out in the bust and taking it in everywhere else.

The first few dresses were a disaster. Jenny nearly busted the zipper of one trying to unsnag it from her bra. And the next one didn't even make it over her boobs. The third one was completely obscene. The fourth one fit, sort of, except it was bright orange and had a ridiculous ruffle running across it, like someone had slashed it with a knife. Jenny poked her head out of the curtain to look for Maureen. Next door, Serena and her mother were just heading out of their dressing room to the cashier's desk.

"Serena!" Jenny called, without thinking twice. Serena turned around and Jenny blushed. She couldn't believe she was talking to Serena van der Woodsen while wearing a bright orange dress with a stupid ruffle on it.

"Hey Jenny," Serena said, beaming sweetly down at her. She walked over and kissed Jenny on both cheeks. Jenny sucked in her breath and gripped the curtain to steady herself. Serena van der Woodsen had just kissed her.

"Wow, crazy dress," Serena said. She leaned in to whisper in Jenny's ear. "You're lucky you don't have your mom with you. I got suckered into buying the ugliest dress in the store." Serena held the dress up. It was long and black and completely gorgeous.

Jenny didn't know what to say. She wished she were the kind of girl who could complain about shopping with her mother. She wished she were the kind of girl who could complain about a beautiful dress being ugly. But she wasn't.

"Is everything all right, dear?" Maureen said, striding over and handing Jenny a strapless bra contraption to try on with her dresses.

Jenny took the bra and glanced at Serena, her cheeks burning. "I'd better keep trying this stuff on," she said. "See you Monday, Serena."

She let the curtain fall closed, but Maureen pulled it open a few inches. "That looks nice," she said, nodding approvingly at the orange dress. "It suits you."

Jenny grimaced. "Does it come in black?" she asked.

"But you're too young for black," Maureen said, frowning.

Jenny frowned back and handed the pile of reject dresses to Maureen, closing the curtain firmly in her face. "Thanks for your help," she called. She yanked the orange dress over her head and whipped off her bra, reaching for a black stretch-satin dress she had picked out herself. Braless, she pulled the dress on over her head and felt it ooze all over her. When she looked up, little Jenny Humphrey had vanished from the dressing room. In her place was a dangerous, slutty sex goddess.

Throw in a pair of kitten heels, a thong, and some Chanel *Vamp* lipstick, and she had it going on. No girl is *ever* too young to wear black.

sunday brunch

Late Sunday morning the steps of the Metropolitan Museum of Art were crawling with people. Tourists, mostly, and locals who had come for a brief visit so they could brag about it to their friends and sound cultured.

Inside, brunch was being served in the Egyptian wing for all the museum's board members and their families. The Egyptian wing was a superb setting for nighttime parties—glittering gold and exotic, with the moonlight shining dramatically through its modern glass walls. But it was all wrong for brunch. Smoked salmon and eggs and mummified Egyptian Pharaohs really don't mix. Plus, the morning sun was shining so brightly through the slanting glass walls, it made even the slightest hangover feel ten times worse.

Who invented brunch anyway? The only decent place to be on Sunday mornings is in bed.

The room was filled with large round tables and freshly-scrubbed Upper-East-Siders. Eleanor Waldorf, Cyrus Rose, the van der Woodsens, the Basses, the Archibalds, and their children were there, all seated around one table. Blair was sitting between Cyrus Rose and her mother, looking grumpy.

Nate had been intermittently baked, drunk, or passed out since Friday, and looked woozy and rumpled, as if he'd just woken up. Serena was wearing some of the new clothes she'd bought shopping with her mother the day before, and she had a new haircut, with soft layers framing her face. She looked even more beautiful than ever, but nervous and jumpy after drinking six cups of coffee. Only Chuck seemed at ease, happily sipping his Bloody Mary.

Cyrus Rose sliced his salmon-and-leek omelet in half and plunked it on a pumpernickel bagel. "I've been craving eggs," he said, biting into it hungrily. "You know when your body tells you you need something?" he said, to no one in particular. "Mine's shouting, 'Eggs, eggs, eggs!'"

And mine's shouting, "Shut the fuck up," Blair thought.

Blair pushed her plate toward him. "Here, have mine. I hate eggs," she said.

Cyrus pushed her plate back. "No, you're growing. You need that more than I do."

"That's right, Blair," her mother agreed. "Eat your eggs. They're good for you."

"I hear eggs make your hair shiny," Misty Bass added.

Blair shook her head. "I don't eat chicken abortions," she said stubbornly. "They make me gag."

Chuck reached across the table. "I'll eat them, if you don't want them."

"Oh, now, Chuck," Mrs. Bass clucked. "Don't be a piggy."

"She said she didn't want them," Chuck said. "Right, Blair?"

Blair handed her plate over, careful not to look at Serena or Nate, sitting on either side of Chuck.

Serena was busy cutting her omelet into little squares,

like Scrabble pieces. She began building tall towers of them.

Out of the corner of his eye, Nate was watching her. He was also watching Chuck's hands. Each time they slid underneath the tablecloth and out of view, Nate imagined them all over Serena's legs.

"Anyone see the Styles section of the *Times* today?" Cyrus asked, looking around the table.

Serena's head shot up. Her picture with the Remi brothers. She'd forgotten all about it.

She pursed her lips and slunk down in her chair, waiting for an inquisition from her parents and everyone else at the table. But it never came. It was part of their social code not to dwell on things that embarrassed them.

"Pass me the cream, Nate darling?" Blair's mother said, while smiling at Serena.

And that was that.

Nate's mother cleared her throat. "How is the *Kiss on the Lips* party going, Blair? Are you girls all ready?" she asked, swigging her Seven-and-Seven.

"Yes, we're all set," Blair answered politely. "We finally got the invitations cleared up. And Kate Spade is sending over the gift bags after school on Thursday."

"I remember all the cotillions I used to organize," Mrs. van der Woodsen said, with a dreamy expression. "But the thing we always used to worry about most was would the boys show up." She smiled at Nate and Chuck. "We don't have to worry about that with you two, do we?" she said.

"I'm all over it," Chuck said, scarfing Blair's omelet.

"I'll be there," Nate said. He glanced at Blair, who was staring at him now.

Nate was wearing that same green cashmere sweater she had given him in Sun Valley. The one with the gold heart.

"Excuse me," Blair said. Then she stood up abruptly and left the table.

Nate followed her.

"Blair!" he called, weaving his way around the other tables, ignoring his friend Jeremy, who was waving to him from across the room. "Wait up."

Without turning around, Blair began walking even faster, her heels clacking on the white marble floor.

They reached the hallway to the restrooms. "Come on, Blair. I'm sorry, okay? Can we please talk?" Nate called.

Blair reached the door to the women's room and turned around, pushing it halfway open with her rear end.

"Just leave me alone, okay?" she said sharply, and went inside.

Nate stood outside the door for a moment with his hands in his pockets, thinking. That morning, when he'd put on the green sweater Blair had given him, he'd found a little gold heart sewn into the sleeve. He'd never noticed it before, but it was obvious Blair had put it there. For the first time, he realized that she really meant it when she'd said she loved him.

It was pretty intense. And pretty flattering. And it kind of made him want her again. It wasn't just any girl who'd sew a gold heart into your clothes.

He had that right.

Serena had to pee desperately, but she couldn't face being in the bathroom at the same time as Blair. After Blair and Nate had been gone for five minutes, though, Serena couldn't hold it any longer. She stood up and headed for the ladies' room.

Familiar faces gazed up at Serena as she passed their tables. A waitress offered her a glass of champagne. But Serena shook her head and hurried down the marble hall to the bathrooms. Quick, heavy footsteps smacked on the floor behind her, and she turned around. It was Cyrus Rose.

"Tell Blair to hurry if she wants dessert, will you?" he told her.

Serena nodded and pushed open the door to the ladies' room. Blair was washing her hands. She looked up, staring at Serena's reflection in the mirror over the sink.

"Cyrus says to hurry if you want dessert," Serena said abruptly, walking into a stall, and banging the door shut. She pulled down her underwear and tried to pee, but she couldn't, not with Blair in the room.

Serena couldn't believe herself. How many times in the past had she and Blair gone to the bathroom together, talking and laughing while they peed? Too many times to count. And now Serena felt so uptight in Blair's presence she couldn't go? It was a total mindfuck.

There was a quiet, awkward pause.

Don't you just *hate* awkward pauses?

"Okay," Serena heard Blair say before she left the bathroom.

The door swung shut and Serena relaxed and started to pee.

Cyrus caught Nate in the men's room.

"You and Blair have a fight?" Cyrus asked. He unzipped his pants and stood at the urinal.

Lucky Nate.

Nate shrugged as he washed his hands. "Kind of," he said.

"Let me guess, it was about sex, right?" Cyrus said.

Nate blushed and pulled a paper towel out of the dispenser. "Well, sort of . . ." he said. He really didn't want to get into it.

Cyrus flushed the urinal and joined Nate at the sinks. He washed his hands and began fussing with his tie, which was bright pink with yellow lions' heads on it. Very Versace.

Read: *tacky*.

"The only thing couples really fight about is sex and money," Cyrus observed.

Nate stood there with his hands in his pockets.

"That's all right, kid. I'm not going to give you a lecture or anything. This is my future stepdaughter we're talking about. I'm sure as hell not going to tell you how to get into her pants."

Cyrus chuckled to himself and left the bathroom, leaving Nate to stare after him. He wondered if Blair knew Cyrus was planning on marrying her mother.

Nate turned on the tap and splashed cold water on his face. He studied himself in the mirror. He'd been up late last night with the boys, playing stupid drinking games to *Tomb Raider*. Every time they saw Angelina Jolie's nipples, they had to drink. He'd tried to drown his thoughts of Blair and Serena in as much booze as he could swallow, and now he was paying for it. His face was pale, there were brownish-purple circles under his eyes, and his cheeks were hollow. He looked like shit.

As soon as this damned brunch was over, he was heading into the park for a smoke in the sun and couple of tall-boys. The perfect cure-all.

But first he'd have to flirt with Blair a little bit. Enough to make her want him again.

Atta boy.

Instead of going back to her table when she left the ladies' room, Blair wound her way across the room, looking for Kati and Isabel's table.

"Blair! Over here!" Kati called, patting the empty chair next to her. Their parents and friends were working the room, socializing, so the girls had the table to themselves.

"Here," Isabel said, handing Blair a glass full of champagne and orange juice.

"Thanks," Blair said, taking a sip.

"Jeremy Scott Tomkinson just came over and tried to get us to come to the park with him," Kati said. She giggled. "He's kind of cute, you know, in a Waspoid kind of way."

Hey, cool word!

Isabel turned to Blair, rolling her eyes. "Isn't this boring? How's your table?"

"Don't ask," Blair said. "Guess who I'm sitting with?"

The other two girls sniggered; they didn't have to guess.

"Have you seen that billboard of her?" Isabel asked Blair.

Blair nodded and rolled her eyes.

"What's it supposed to be, anyway?" Kati said. "Her belly button?"

Blair still had no idea. "Who cares?"

"She has no shame," Isabel ventured. "I actually feel kind of sorry for her."

"Me too," Kati agreed.

"Well, don't," Blair said fiercely.

Grrr.

Nate pushed open the men's room door at exactly the same time that Serena pushed open the ladies'. Together, they walked down the hallway back to the table.

"Nate," Serena said, smoothing her new brown suede skirt over her legs. "Can you please explain why you're not talking to me?"

"I'm not not talking to you," Nate said. "See, I'm talking to you right now."

"Barely," Serena said. "What happened? What's wrong? Did Blair say something to you about me?"

Instinctively, Nate reached into his jacket pocket and fingered the flask of whiskey that was hidden there. He looked down at the marble floor, avoiding Serena's beautiful sad eyes.

"We should get back," Nate said, speeding up.

"Fine," Serena answered, trailing after him slowly.

She had that sour salty taste in the back of her throat again, the taste of tears. She'd been holding them back for too many days now, and she could feel a tidal wave coming on. All of a sudden she would start sobbing, and she wouldn't be able to stop.

When Nate and Serena took their places at the table, Chuck smirked at them knowingly. *How was it?* his face seemed to say. Serena wanted to hit him.

She ordered another cup of coffee and dumped four teaspoons of sugar in it and stirred and stirred, like she was trying to stir a hole through the cup, the saucer, the table, and the floor, burrowing her way into some old pharaoh's tomb where she could cry and cry and no one would find her.

Nate ordered a Bloody Mary.

"Bottoms up!" Chuck said cheerfully, banging his glass against Nate's and taking a big gulp.

Blair was back at the table. She had already devoured her crème brulée and was working on her mother's. It was full of chicken abortions, but she didn't care—she was going to throw it all up in a minute anyway.

"Hey Blair," Nate said softly, causing Blair to drop her spoon with a clatter. He smiled and leaned across the table. "That looks awesome," he said. "Can I have a bite?"

Blair's hand fluttered nervously to her heart. Sexy Nate. Her Nate. God, she wanted him. But she wasn't going to give up that easily. She had her pride.

Blair regained her composure and pushed her plate toward him, reaching for her drink and downing the rest of it in one big swallow. "You can have the rest," she said, and stood up. "Excuse me." Then she clacked away in her heels to stick her finger down her throat in the ladies' room.

Some lady.

Disclaimer: All the real names of places, people, and events have been altered or abbreviated to protect the innocent. Namely, me.

hey people!

I thought **S** looked cute in her picture in the Sunday *Times* Styles section. Although her teachers probably weren't thrilled to see her double-fisting martinis on a school day. To tell you the truth, I'm kind of over the whole thing. I mean, isn't it enough that we have to see that picture of her every time we use public transportation? Obviously *you're* not over it yet, though.

Your E-mail

Q:
hey gg,
i went to the show at the gallery and looked for ur picture. very sexy. i like ur column too. u rule.
—Bigfan

A:
Dear Bigfan,
As long as you are not a stalker, I guess I'm flattered.
—GG

Q:
Dear Gossip Girl,
When I saw **S**'s picture in the paper, I had an idea!! Are you **S**? If you are, you are very sneaky. Also, my dad loves you and wants you to write a book. He's got lots of connections. If you tell me who you are, he can make you famous.

—JNYHY

A:
Hey JNYHY,
You are very sneaky yourself. And not to brag or anything, but I'm already kind of famous. Infamous is more like it. All the more reason for me not to tell you who I am.
—GG

Sightings

D was seen returning a gorgeous **Armani** tux at **Barneys** and renting a much less gorgeous one at a formal store. His sister *J* was seen buying underwear at **La Petite Coquette**, although she chickened out on the thong. *N* was seen buying a big bag of pot in Central Park. Tell me something new. *B* was seen in the **J. Sisters** salon getting another Brazilian wax. The old one must have started to itch. *S* was seen with her feet out her bedroom window, letting her toenails dry. I don't think she's ever spent this much time at home in her entire life. Maybe she should get a cat or something. Meow.

TWO QUESTIONS

First: If you knew about a party that you weren't invited to, wouldn't you go, just to piss people off? I would.

Second: If you'd made up your mind to go to the party, wouldn't you want to really rub people's noses in it by looking completely gorgeous and stealing everyone's boyfriends? *Definitely.*

But who knows what *S* will decide to do. That girl is full of surprises. . . .

At least I've given us all something to think about while we're getting our pedicures, plucking our eyebrows, and squeezing our zits.

See you at the party!

You know you love me,

gossip girl

a change of heart

"Ugly, ugly, ugly," Serena said, wadding her new black dress into a ball and tossing it onto her bed.

A gorgeous Tocca dress? Come on, how ugly could it be?

Each day that week, Serena had dressed in her maroon uniform, gone to school, come home, watched some TV, eaten dinner, watched some more TV, and gone to sleep. She even did some homework. She spoke to no one except her parents and her teachers and maybe a passing greeting to the girls at school. She was beginning to feel only half-there, like the shadow of her former self, a girl people had known once, but couldn't quite remember anymore. And for the first time in her entire life, she felt ugly and awkward. Her eyes and hair looked dull to her, and her beautiful smile and cool demeanor had been roped off until further notice.

Now it was Friday, the night of the *Kiss on the Lips* party. And the question she couldn't answer: to go or not to go?

It used to be, before fancy parties like this, Serena and her friends would spend half the night getting dressed together—swilling gin-and-tonics, dancing around in their underwear, trying on crazy outfits. But tonight Serena rummaged through her closet alone.

There was the pair of jeans with the rip in the leg where she'd snagged them on a barbed-wire fence in Ridgefield. There was the white satin dress she'd worn to the Christmas dance in ninth grade. Her brother's old leather jacket. Her moldy tennis shoes that should have been thrown out two years ago. And what was this? A red wool sweater—Nate's. Serena held it to her face and smelled it. It smelled like her, not him.

Toward the back of the closet was a black velvet flapper dress that Serena had bought with Blair at a vintage store. It was a dress to wear while drinking and dancing and lounging around decoratively in a huge house full of people having a good time. It reminded Serena of the good-time gal she'd been when she bought the dress—her old self, the girl she'd been up until two weeks ago. She let her robe drop to the floor and slipped the dress on over her head. Maybe it would give her back some of her power.

Barefoot, she padded into her parents' dressing room, where they were getting ready for their own black-tie affair.

"What do you think?" Serena asked, doing a little twirl in front of them.

"Oh, Serena, you're not wearing *that*. Tell me you're not," her mother exclaimed, fastening a long rope of pearls around her neck.

"What's wrong with it?" Serena said.

"It's an old ratty thing," Mrs. van der Woodsen told her. "It's just the sort of dress my grandmother was buried in."

"What's wrong with one of those outfits you bought with your mother last weekend?" Mr. van der Woodsen suggested. "Didn't you buy anything to wear to the party?"

"Of course she did," Mrs. van der Woodsen said. "She bought a lovely black dress."

"That makes me look like a fat nun," Serena said grumpily.

She put her hands on her hips and posed in front of her mother's full-length mirror. "I like this dress. It's got character."

Her mother sighed disapprovingly. "Well, what's Blair wearing?" she asked.

Serena stared at her mother and blinked. Under normal circumstances she would have known exactly what Blair was wearing, down to her underwear. And Blair would have insisted on going shoe-shopping together, because if you bought a new dress, you had to have a pair of new shoes. Blair loved shoes.

"Blair told everyone to wear vintage," Serena lied.

Her mother was about to respond when Serena heard her phone ring in her bedroom. Was it Nate calling to apologize? Blair? She raced down the hall in her bare feet, scrambling to pick it up.

"Hello?" she said breathlessly.

"Yo, bitch. Sorry I haven't called in a while."

Serena took a deep breath and sat down on her bed. It was Erik, her brother.

"Hey," she said.

"Saw you in the paper last Sunday. You are crazy, aren't you?" Erik laughed. "What did Mom say?"

"Nothing. It's like I can do whatever I want now. Everyone thinks I'm like, *ruined* or something," Serena said, fumbling for the right words.

"That's not true," Erik said. "Hey, what's up? You sound sad."

"Yeah," Serena said. Her lower lip started to tremble. "I sort of am."

"How come? What's going on?"

"I don't know. There's this party I'm supposed to go to that everyone's going to. You know how it is," she began.

"That doesn't sound so bad," Erik said gently.

Serena propped her pillows against the headboard of her bed and wriggled under her comforter. She rested her head against the pillows and closed her eyes. "It's just that no one's talking to me anymore. I don't even know why, but ever since I've been back it's been like I have mad cow disease or something," she explained. The tears began to fall from underneath her closed lids.

"What about Blair and Nate? Those guys must be talking to you," Erik said. "They're your best friends."

"Not anymore," Serena said quietly. Tears were streaming freely down her face now. She picked up a pillow and dabbed it against her cheeks to ebb the flow.

"Well, you know what I say?" Erik said.

Serena swallowed and wiped her nose on the back of her hand. "What?"

"Fuck 'em. Totally. You don't need them. You're like, the coolest chick in the Western Hemisphere. Fuck 'em, fuck 'em, fuck 'em," he said.

"Yeah," Serena said dubiously. "But they're my friends."

"Not anymore. You just said so yourself. You can get new friends. I'm serious," Erik said. "You can't let assholes turn you into an asshole. You just have to fuck 'em."

It was a perfect Erikism. Serena laughed, wiped her runny nose on a pillow, and threw it across the room. "Okay," she said, sitting up. "You're right."

"I'm always right. That's why I'm so hard to get ahold of. There's a huge demand for people like me," he said.

"I miss you," Serena told him, chewing on her pinky nail.

"I miss you too," Erik said.

"Serena? We're leaving!" she heard her mother call from out in the hall.

"Okay, I better go," Serena said. "Love you."

"Bye."

Serena clicked off. On the end of her bed was the invitation to the *Kiss on the Lips* party that Jenny had made for her. She snatched it up and tossed it in her wastepaper basket.

Erik was right. She didn't have to go to some stupid benefit just because everyone else was going. They didn't even want her there. Fuck 'em. She was free to do what she pleased.

She carried the phone over to her desk and shuffled through a pile of papers until she found the Constance Billard School student directory, which had arrived in the mail on Monday. Serena read through the names. She wasn't the only one skipping the party. She could find someone else to hang out with.

the red or the black

"Yo," Vanessa said, picking up the phone. She was getting ready to go out with her sister and her friends, and she was wearing a black bra, black jeans, and her Doc Martens. She didn't have any clean black shirts left, and her sister was trying to convince her to wear a red one.

"Hi. Is that Vanessa Abrams?" a girl's voice said on the other end of the phone.

"Yes. Who's this?" Vanessa said, standing in front of her bedroom mirror and holding the red shirt up to her chest. She hadn't worn any color but black in two years. Why should she start now? *Please*. It's not like wearing a red shirt was going turn her into a bouncy cheerleader with blond pigtails. She'd have to be brainwashed for that to happen.

"It's Serena van der Woodsen."

Vanessa stopped looking at herself and threw the shirt on her bed. "Oh," she said. "What's up?"

"Well," Serena said. "I totally understand why you wanted to cast Marjorie. You know, for your film? But you seem to really know what you're doing, and I really need the extracurricular or Ms. Glos is going to kill me. So I thought I'd try to make my own movie."

"Uh huh," Vanessa said, trying to figure out why Serena van der Woodsen of all people would be calling her up on a Friday night. Didn't she have a ball to go to or something? Some fête?

"So anyway, I was wondering if maybe you could help me. You know, like show me how to use the camera, and whatever. I mean, I really don't know what I'm doing," Serena said. She sighed. "I don't know, maybe making a film is a dumb idea. It's probably a lot harder than I think."

"It's not dumb," Vanessa said, feeling kind of sorry for Serena despite herself. "I can show you some of the basic stuff."

"Really?" Serena said. She sounded thrilled. "How about tomorrow? Can you do it tomorrow?"

Saturday was Vanessa's vampire day. She usually woke up after dark and then went to the diner or to the movies with her sister or Dan.

"Sunday is better," she said.

"Okay. Sunday," Serena said. "You probably have a lot of equipment and stuff at your house, right? Why don't I come over there, so you don't have to lug it around."

"Sounds good," Vanessa said.

"Okay," Serena said. She paused. She didn't seem very eager to hang up the phone.

"Hey, isn't that big party in the old Barneys building tonight?" Vanessa said. "Aren't you going?"

"Nah," Serena answered. "I wasn't invited."

Vanessa nodded, processing this information. Serena van der Woodsen wasn't invited? Maybe she wasn't so bad after all.

"Well, do you want to come out with us tonight?" Vanessa offered before she could stop herself. "Me and my big sister are going to a bar here in Williamsburg. Her band is playing."

"I'd love to," Serena said.

Vanessa gave her the address of The Five and Dime—the bar her sister was playing in—and hung up the phone.

Life was so strange. One day you could be picking your nose and eating donuts, and the next day you could be hanging out with Serena van der Woodsen. She picked up the red shirt, pulled it on over her head, and looked in the mirror. She looked like a tulip. A tulip with a stubbly black head.

"Dan will like it," her sister Ruby told her, standing in the doorway. She handed Vanessa a tube of dark red lipstick. *Vamp.*

"Well, Dan's not coming out tonight," Vanessa said, smirking at her sister. She dabbed on the lipstick and rubbed her lips together. "He has to take his little sister to some fancy ball."

She checked herself out in the mirror once more. The lipstick made her big brown eyes look even bigger, and the shirt was kind of cool, in a loud, look-at-me way.

Vanessa stuck out her chest and smiled invitingly at her reflection. *Maybe I'll get lucky*, she thought. Or maybe not.

"I have a friend coming to meet us," Vanessa informed her sister.

"Boy or girl?" Ruby asked, turning around to check out her butt in the mirror.

"Girl."

"Name?" said Ruby.

"Serena van der Woodsen," Vanessa mumbled.

"The girl whose picture is all over town?" Ruby said, clearly delighted.

"Yeah, that's her," Vanessa said.

"Well, I bet she's pretty cool," Ruby said, rubbing hair gel into her thick black bangs.

"Maybe," Vanessa replied. "I guess we'll find out."

kiss on the lips

"What fantastic flowers," said Becky Dormand, a junior at Constance. She kissed Blair on both cheeks. "And what a hot dress!"

"Thanks, Beck," Blair said, looking down at the green satin sheath she was wearing. She had gotten her period that morning, but she had to wear extremely flimsy underwear with her dress. It made her nervous.

A waiter walked past with a tray of champagne. Blair whisked a flute off his tray and downed it in a matter of seconds. It was her third so far.

"I love your shoes," Blair said. Becky was wearing black, high-heeled sandals that laced all the way up to her knees. They went perfectly with her short black tutu dress and her super-high ponytail. She looked like a ballerina on acid.

"I can't wait for the gift bags," Laura Salmon squealed. "Kate Spade, right?"

"I heard they even put a glow-in-the-dark condom in them," Rain Hoffstetter giggled. "Isn't that cool?"

"Not that you'll be using it or anything," Blair said.

"How do *you* know?" Rain huffed.

"Blair?" Blair heard someone say in a tremulous voice.

Blair turned around to see little Jenny Humphrey standing behind her, looking like a human Wonderbra in her black satin dress.

"Oh, hello," Blair said coolly. "Thanks again for doing those invitations. They really came out great."

"Thanks for *letting* me do them," Jenny said. Her eyes darted around the huge room, which was throbbing with people and music and smoke. Black three-foot-high candles in tall glass beakers trimmed with peacock feathers and fragrant white orchids flickered everywhere. Jenny had never been to anything this cool in her life. "God, I don't know anyone here," she said nervously.

"You don't?" Blair said. She wondered if Jenny thought she was going to talk to *her* all night.

"No. My brother Dan was supposed to come with me, but he didn't really want to, so I just let him drop me off. Actually, I do know one person," Jenny said.

"Oh," said Blair. "And who is that?"

"Serena van der Woodsen," Jenny chirped. "We're making a movie together. Did she tell you?"

Just then, a waitress brandished a platter of sushi under Blair's nose. Blair grabbed a chunky tuna roll and shoved it into her mouth. "Serena's not here yet," she said, chewing hungrily. "But I'm sure she'll be thrilled to see you."

"Okay. I guess I'll just wait for her here, then," Jenny said, snagging two flutes of champagne from a waiter's tray. She handed one to Blair. "Will you wait with me?"

Blair took the champagne, tilted her head back, and poured it down the hatch. The sickly sweet fizziness of it didn't exactly jive with the raw fish and seaweed she'd just eaten. Blair burped queasily.

"I'll be right back," she told Jenny, practically running for the powder room.

Jenny took a sip of her champagne and gazed up at the crystal chandelier hanging from the ceiling, congratulating herself on making it in there. This was exactly what she'd always wanted. She closed her eyes and finished off her flute of champagne. When she opened her eyes again, she saw stars, but still no Serena.

Another waiter walked by with more champagne, and Jenny took two more glasses. She'd drunk a little beer and wine at home with her dad, but she'd never had champagne before. It tasted wonderful.

Careful, it doesn't taste so wonderful when you're on your knees in the bathroom, throwing it up.

Jenny looked around for Blair again, but couldn't find her. The party was so crowded, and although she recognized a lot of faces, there was no one she'd actually feel comfortable going up and talking to. But Serena would be there soon, she had to be.

Jenny walked over to the bottom step of a marble staircase and sat down. She could see everything from there, including the door. She waited, drinking both glasses of champagne and wishing her dress wasn't so tight. It was starting to make her feel nauseous.

"Well, *hello*," a deep voice said, hovering above her.

Jenny looked up. Her eyes settled on Chuck Bass's after-shave-commercial face and she sucked in her breath. He was the best-looking boy she'd ever seen, and he was looking right at her.

"Aren't you going to introduce me?" Chuck said, staring at Jenny's chest.

"To who?" Jenny said, frowning.

Chuck just laughed and held out his hand. Blair had sent him over there to talk to some chick, and he'd been skeptical. But not anymore. The cleavage on her! It was definitely his lucky night.

"I'm Chuck. Would you like to dance?"

Jenny hesitated and glanced at the door. Still no Serena. Then she shifted her gaze back to Chuck. She couldn't believe a handsome and self-assured boy like him would want to dance with *her*. But she wasn't wearing a sexy black dress just to sit on the steps all night. She stood up, a little wobblier than she'd been before, after so much champagne.

"Sure, let's dance," she slurred, falling against Chuck's chest.

He slipped his arm around her waist and squeezed her tight. "Good girl," he said, like he was talking to a dog.

As she stumbled out onto the dance floor with him Jenny realized Chuck hadn't even asked her her name. But he was so handsome, and the party was so amazing. This would definitely go down as one of the most memorable nights of her life.

Yes. It would.

the five and dime

"I always drink rum and Coke," Vanessa told Serena. "Unless I'm doing shots. But you have whatever you want. They have everything here."

Ruby was taking their drink order. Because she was in the band, she got them for free.

"I feel like something different," Serena mused. "Can I just get a shot of Stoli and a Coke on the side?" she asked Ruby.

"Nice choice," Ruby said approvingly. Ruby had a cool black bob with short bangs and was wearing dark green leather pants. She looked like the kind of girl who could take care of herself anywhere, anytime. Her band was called SugarDaddy, and she was the only girl in it. She played bass.

"And don't forget my cherry!" Vanessa yelled after her as Ruby left to get the drinks.

"Your sister's awesome," Serena said.

Vanessa shrugged. "Yeah," she said. "It's a pain in my ass, though. I mean, everyone's always like, 'Ruby's so cool' and I'm like, 'Hello?'"

Serena laughed. "I know what you mean. My older brother—he goes to Brown, and everybody loves him. My parents are always so into everything he does, and now that I'm back from boarding school it's like, 'Oh, we have a daughter?'"

"Totally," Vanessa agreed. She couldn't believe she was having such a ridiculously normal conversation with Serena van der Woodsen.

Ruby brought them their drinks. "Sorry guys, I gotta go set up," she said.

"Good luck," Serena told her.

"Thanks, sweetie," Ruby said. She picked up her guitar case and went to find her bandmates.

Vanessa couldn't believe it. Ruby never called anyone sweetie except for Tofu, her parakeet. Serena certainly had a way of melting people's hearts. Vanessa was even starting to like her a little herself. She picked up her drink and clinked glasses with Serena. "To cool-ass chicks," she said, knowing it sounded seriously gay, but not really giving a shit.

Serena laughed and tossed back her shot of Stoli. She wiped her eyes and blinked a few times. A scruffy-looking guy wearing an oversized tuxedo was walking into the bar. He stopped in the doorway and stared at Serena as if he'd seen a ghost.

"Hey, isn't that your friend Dan?" Serena asked Vanessa, pointing at him.

Dan was wearing a tuxedo for the first time in his life. He'd felt pretty sharp when he first put it on, but he still couldn't deal with the *Kiss on the Lips* party. So when Jenny let him blow the party off, he'd come to The Five and Dime to apologize to Vanessa for being such a dick over the Marjorie thing.

He'd tried to convince himself it didn't matter that he'd probably never see Serena van der Woodsen again in his life. After all, he told himself, life was fragile and absurd.

Life was absurd all right. Because *there Serena was*. In Williamsburg, of all places. His dream girl.

Dan felt like Cinderella. He shoved his hands in his pockets to keep them from shaking, and tried to plan his next move. He would walk over and suavely offer to buy Serena a drink. Too bad the only suave thing about him was his outfit. Even it was only half as suave as it could have been if he'd kept the Armani from Barneys.

"Hey," Dan said when he reached their table, his voice cracking.

"What're you doing here?" Vanessa said. She couldn't believe her luck. Did it have to be quite this bad? Was she going to have to sit there for the rest of the night watching Dan drool over Serena?

Sorry, honey.

"I blew off that *Kiss on the Lips* party. It really wasn't my thing," Dan said.

"Me too," Serena said, smiling at Dan like he'd never been smiled at before.

Dan clutched the back of Vanessa's chair for balance. "Hey," he said shyly.

"You remember Serena," Vanessa said. "She's in my class at Constance."

"Hey Dan," Serena said. "Nice tux."

Dan blushed and looked down at himself. "Thanks," he said. He looked up again. "And that dress is . . . looks . . . pretty also," he stuttered. He hadn't thought it was possible to sound so idiotic.

"What about *my* shirt?" Vanessa said loudly. "Have you ever seen me look this hot?"

Dan stared at Vanessa's shirt. It was a red T-shirt. Not very exciting. "Is it new?" he asked, confused.

"Never mind," Vanessa sighed, impatiently swirling the maraschino cherry around in her glass.

"Grab a chair," Serena said, moving over to make room for him. "Ruby's band is going to play in a minute."

The rumors couldn't possibly be true. Serena didn't look like a sex-crazed, drug-addicted maniac. She looked delicate and perfect and exciting, like a wildflower you stumble upon unexpectedly in Central Park. Dan wanted to hold hands with her and whisper to each other all night long.

He sat down next to her. His hands were shaking so badly he had to sit on them to keep them still. He wanted her so badly.

The band started to play.

Serena finished her vodka.

"Would you like another one?" Dan offered eagerly.

Serena shook her head. "I'm okay," she said, sitting back in her chair. "Let's just listen to the music for a while."

"Okay," Dan said. As long as he was near her, he'd do anything.

as usual, *b* is in the bathroom and *n* is stoned

"Hello, everyone!" Jeremy Scott Tompkinson said loudly, throwing open the doors to the old Barneys building.

As always, Nate, Jeremy, Anthony, and Charlie had smoked a big fatty before the party. Nate was silly high, and when he walked through the door and saw Blair pushing her way through the crowd with her hand pressed over her mouth, he started to giggle.

"What're you laughing at, jackass?" Anthony said, shoving his elbow into Nate's ribs. "Nothing's even happened yet."

Nate wiped his hand over his face and tried to look serious, but it was hard to keep a straight face in a room full of boys dressed like penguins, and girls in sexy dresses. He knew Blair was in the bathroom, throwing up as usual. The question was, should he go rescue her? It was the type of thing a good, concerned boyfriend would do.

Go for it. You know you want to.

"Bar's over there," Charlie said, leading the way.

"I'll catch you guys later," Nate said, pushing his way through the crowded dance floor.

He ducked around Chuck, who was gyrating his crotch against the ass of a short girl with curly brown hair and insane cleavage, and headed for the ladies room.

★　　　★　　　★

But Blair hadn't made it to the ladies' room. Before she'd gotten there, a middle-aged woman in a red Chanel suit with a "Save the Falcons" button pinned to it had stopped her.

"Blair Waldorf?" the woman said, holding out her hand and smiling her best fundraising smile. "I'm Rebecca Agnelli, from the Central Park Save the Peregrine Falcon Foundation."

Talk about bad timing.

Blair stared at the woman's hand. Her own right hand was clapped over her mouth, holding in the vomit that threatened to spew out at any moment. She started to remove it so she could shake hands, but then a waiter walked by with sizzling skewers of spicy chicken, and Blair gagged.

Blair squeezed her lips together to keep the puke from seeping out the sides of her mouth and changed hands, clapping the left one over her mouth and reaching out to shake hands with her right hand.

"It's so wonderful to finally meet you," the woman said as they clasped hands. "I can't thank you enough for all you've done."

Blair nodded and pulled her hand away. Enough was enough. She couldn't hold on any longer. Her eyes darted around the crowded room, desperately seeking help.

There were Kati and Isabel, dancing with each other. There was Anthony Avuldsen, handing out tabs of E. There was Jeremy Scott Tompkinson, trying to teach Laura Salmon and Rain Hoffstetter how to blow smoke rings by the bar. There was Chuck, holding that little Ginny girl so tight it looked like her boobs might explode.

All the extras were there, but where was her leading man, her savior?

"Blair?"

She turned around and saw Nate pushing his way through

the crowd toward her. Nate's eyes were bloodshot, his face slack, his hair uncombed. He looked more like a forgettable supporting actor than a leading man.

Was this all there was? Was Nate *it*?

Blair didn't have much choice. She opened her eyes wide, silently asking Nate for help and praying he'd be up to the job.

Ms. Agnelli frowned and turned around to see what Blair was staring at. Blair made a run for it, and Nate stepped in just in time.

Thank God he was so stoned.

"Nate Archibald," Nate said, shaking hands with the woman. "My mother is a big fan of those falcons."

Ms. Agnelli laughed and blushed a little. What a charming young man. "Well, of course she is," she said. "Your family has been very generous with our foundation."

Nate plucked two flutes of champagne off a passing tray and handed one to her. He raised his glass. "To the birds," he said, clinking his glass with hers and trying to fend off an outbreak of the giggles.

Ms. Agnelli blushed again. This boy was too cute!

"Hey, those two girls helped plan the party, too," Nate said, pointing at Kati and Isabel, who were standing on the edge of the dance floor, useless as usual. He waved them over.

"Hello, Nate," said Kati, tottering over on four-inch stilettos.

Isabel clutched her drink and stared at the strange woman standing next to Nate. "Hi," she said. "I *love* your suit."

"Thank you, dear. I'm Rebecca Agnelli, from the Central Park Save the Peregrine Falcons Foundation," the woman said. She held her hand out to Isabel, who reached out with both arms to give her a drunken hug.

"Excuse me," said Nate, bowing out right on cue.

★　　　★　　　★

"Blair?" Nate called, cautiously pushing open the ladies' room door. "Are you in there?"

Blair was crouched in the end stall. "Shit," she said softly, wiping her mouth with toilet paper. She stood up and flushed. "I'll be right out," she said, waiting for him to leave.

But Nate pushed the ladies' room door open all the way and stepped inside. On a counter by the sinks were little bottles of Evian, perfume, hairspray, Advil, and hand lotion. He unscrewed a bottle of water and shook a couple Advil onto his palm.

Blair opened the stall door. "You're still here," she said.

Nate handed her the pills and the water. "I'm still here," he repeated.

Blair swallowed the pills, sipping the water slowly. "I'm really fine," she said. "You can go back to the party."

"You look nice," Nate said, ignoring her. He reached out and rubbed one of Blair's bare shoulders. Her skin felt warm and soft, and Nate wished they could lie down on her bed and fall asleep together like they always used to.

"Thanks," said Blair, her lower lip beginning to tremble. "So do you."

"I'm sorry, Blair. I really am," Nate began.

Blair nodded and began to cry. Nate pulled a paper towel from the dispenser and handed it to her.

"I think the only real reason I did it . . . I mean, that I did it with Serena . . . is because I knew she'd do it," he said, grasping for the right words. "But it was you I wanted all along."

Nice one.

Blair swallowed. He'd said it just right, exactly the way she'd written it in the script in her head. She put her arms around Nate's neck and let him hold her. His clothes smelled like pot.

Nate pushed her away and looked down into her eyes. "So everything is okay now?" he said. "You still want me?"

Blair caught the reflection of the two of them together in the bathroom mirror and gazed up into Nate's gorgeous green eyes and nodded yes.

"But only if you promise to stay away from Serena," she sniffled.

Nate wound a strand of Blair's hair around his finger and breathed in the scent of her perfume. It felt okay, standing there, holding her. It felt like something he could do. For now, and maybe forever. He didn't need Serena.

He nodded. "I promise."

And then they kissed—a sad, soft kiss. In her head, Blair could hear the swell of music signaling the end of the scene. It had started out a little rocky, but at least the ending was okay.

"Come on," she said, pulling away and wiping the mascara smudges from under her eyes. "Let's go see who's here."

Holding hands, they left the ladies' room. Kati Farkas smiled knowingly as she tottered past them on the way in.

"You guys," she scolded. "Get a room!"

s and d get down

"This band rocks!" Serena shouted at Vanessa over the pounding drum and bass. She wriggled her butt from side to side in her chair, her eyes shining. Dan was having trouble breathing normally. He'd barely touched his drink.

Vanessa smiled, pleased that Serena liked the music. Personally, she hated it, although she'd never tell her sister Ruby that. SugarDaddy was all about people dancing and sweating and shaking their bodies around, which was definitely not Vanessa's thing.

She'd rather lie around in the dark listening to Gregorian chants or whatever. *Yeehaw!*

"Come on," Serena said, standing up. "Let's dance."

Vanessa shook her head. "That's okay," she said. "You go."

"Dan?" Serena said, tugging on his jacket sleeve. "Come on!"

Dan never, ever danced. He was bad at it, and it made him feel like a goofball. He hesitated, glancing at Vanessa, who raised her black eyebrows, challenging him. *If you get up and dance right now, you will go straight to the top of my loser list,* her look said.

Dan stood up. "Sure, why not," he said.

Serena grabbed his hand and pushed her way into the gyrating throng with Dan stumbling after her. Then Serena began to dance, her arms raised over her head, kicking her feet out in front of her and shaking her shoulders. She definitely knew how to dance.

Dan nodded his head up and down and waggled his knees in time to the beat, watching her.

Serena reached out and clasped Dan's hips, rocking them back and forth and around and around, mimicking what her hips were doing all on their own. Dan laughed and Serena smiled and closed her eyes, getting seriously down. Dan closed his eyes too, letting his body follow hers. It really didn't matter that he danced like a moron, or that he was the only one in the room wearing a tuxedo—probably the only one in Williamsburg. He was *with her*, and that was what mattered.

Alone at the table, Vanessa finished first her drink and then Dan's. Then she got up and went to sit down at the bar.

"Nice shirt," the bartender remarked when he saw her. He was in his early twenties, with red hair, long sideburns, and a cute, sly smile. Her sister was always talking about how cute he was.

"Thanks," Vanessa said, smiling back at him. "It's new."

"You should wear red more often," he said. He held his hand out. "I'm Clark. You're Vanessa, right? Ruby's sister?"

Vanessa nodded. She wondered if he was just being nice to her because he liked her sister.

"Can I tell you a secret?" Clark said. He poured a few different things into a martini shaker and shook it up.

Oh, fuck, Vanessa thought. *Here's when he pours out his heart and tells me all about how he's been in love with Ruby forever, but she doesn't seem to notice him. And he wants me to play Cupid and blah, blah, blah.*

"What?" she said.

"Well," Clark said. "I see you and Ruby come in here all the time."

Here he goes, thought Vanessa.

"And you never come up to the bar and talk to me. But I've kind of had a crush on you since I first saw you."

Vanessa stared at him. Was he joking?

Clark poured the drink out of the martini shaker into a short little glass and squeezed a few limes into it. He pushed it toward her. "Try that," he said. "It's on the house."

Vanessa picked up the glass and tasted it. It tasted sweet and sour at the same time, and she couldn't taste any alcohol in it at all. It was good.

"What's it called?" she said.

"Kiss me," Clark said, with an absolutely straight face.

Vanessa put the drink down and leaned over the bar. Serena and Dan could dance their pretty asses off for all she cared. She was about to be kissed.

The *Kiss on the Lips* DJ had just broken up with her boyfriend of four years and was playing sad, slow, love songs back to back. Gorgeously dressed couples held onto each other and swayed to the lonesome riffs, barely moving beneath the soft lights. The air smelled of orchids and candle wax and raw fish and cigarette smoke, and there was a peaceful sophistication to the evening that was both unexpected and familiar. It wasn't the rocking slam-fest that some had hoped for, but it wasn't a bad party, either. There was still plenty of booze left, nothing had caught fire, and the cops hadn't shown up to card people. Besides, the year was just getting started—there were tons more parties to look forward to.

Nate and Blair were dancing together, her cheek against his chest, both of their eyes closed, his lips brushing the top of her head. Blair had put her brain on pause, and her head was full of static. She was tired of dreaming up movies. Right now, real life suited her just fine.

A few couples away, Chuck had his hands full of Jenny Humphrey. Jenny wished the DJ would bring up the tempo. She was trying to dance as fast as she could, to keep Chuck from groping her, but it was having the opposite effect. Every time she moved her shoulders, her boobs bounced out of her dress and practically hit him in the face.

Chuck was absolutely delighted. He put his arms around Jenny's waist and pulled her close, dancing off the dance floor and into the ladies' room.

"What are we doing?" Jenny said, confused. She gazed up into his eyes. She knew Chuck was friends with Serena and Blair, and she wanted to trust him. But Chuck still hadn't asked her what her name was. He'd barely spoken to her at all.

"I just want to kiss you," Chuck said. He bent his head down and enveloped her mouth in his, pressing his tongue against her teeth with such force that she let out a little gasp. Jenny opened her mouth and let him thrust his tongue deep into her throat. She had kissed boys before, playing games at parties. But she'd never tongue kissed like this. *Is this what it's supposed to feel like?* she wondered, suddenly feeling a little frightened. She reached up and pushed against Chuck's chest, pulling her head away from him, desperate for air.

"I have to go to the bathroom," she mumbled, stumbling backwards into a stall and locking the door.

She could see Chuck's feet, standing outside the stall.

"All right," he said. "But I'm not finished with you yet."

Jenny sat down on the toilet seat without pulling up her dress and pretended to pee. Then she stood up and flushed.

"All done?" Chuck called.

Jenny didn't answer. Her mind was racing. What should she do? Anxiously, she reached inside her little black handbag for her cell phone.

Chuck crouched down to look under the stall door. What was she doing in there, the little tease? He crawled forward on his hands and knees. "All right," he said. "That's it, I'm coming in."

Jenny closed her eyes and backed against the stall wall. Quickly, she pressed the buttons for Dan's number into her cell phone, praying that he'd answer.

Ruby's band was playing their last song, and Serena and Dan were slick with sweat. Dan had some new moves down, and he was in the middle of an experimental slide to the side with a pelvic thrust when his cell phone went off.

"Damn," he said, pulling it out of his pocket. He flipped it open.

"Dan," he heard his sister's voice. "I—"

"Hey Jen. Hold on, all right? I can't hear you." He tapped Serena on the arm and pointed to his phone. "Sorry," he shouted over the music. He walked back to the table and put his hand over his free ear. "Jenny?"

"Dan?" Jenny said. Her voice sounded very small and scared and far away. "I need your help. Please come get me?"

"Now?" Dan said. He looked up. Serena was walking toward him, a worried frown on her perfect face.

"Is everything okay?" she mouthed.

"Please, Dan?" Jenny pleaded. She sounded really upset.

"What's wrong?" Dan asked his sister. "Can't you take a cab?"

"No, I—" Jenny said, her voice trailing off. "Just please come, okay, Dan?" she finished hurriedly. And then she hung up.

"Who was that?" Serena said.

"My little sister," Dan told her. "She's at that party. She wants me to come get her."

"Are you going?"

"Yeah, I think I'd better. She sounded kind of weird," he said.

"I'll come with you," Serena offered.

"All right," Dan said, smiling shyly. This night was getting better and better. "That would be cool."

"We'd better tell Vanessa," Serena said, heading for the bar.

Dan followed her. He'd forgotten all about Vanessa. But she looked like she was having a good time talking to the bartender.

"Hey Vanessa," Serena said, touching Vanessa's arm. "Dan just got a call from his sister at the party. He has to go get her."

Vanessa turned around slowly. She was waiting for Clark's eyes to settle on Serena. For his eyeballs to suddenly register "beautiful girl" in bold black letters like the cherries in a slot machine. But Clark only glanced at Serena like she was just another customer.

"What can I get you?" he said, slapping a cocktail napkin down on the bar in front of her.

"Oh, nothing, thanks," Serena said. She turned to Vanessa. "I think I'm going to go with Dan."

"Hey Serena, we better take off," Dan called urgently from behind them.

Vanessa turned around to look at him, waiting so eagerly for Serena. His tongue was practically hanging out of his mouth.

"Okay, have a good rest of the night," Serena said. She leaned over and gave Vanessa a kiss on her cheek. "Tell Ruby I thought she was awesome." Then she slipped away to join Dan.

"See you, Vanessa," Dan called, turning to go.

Vanessa turned back to Clark without a word. She couldn't wait to kiss him again, and forget all about Serena and Dan, heading off into the night together.

"Who were they?" Clark said, resting his elbows on the bar. He picked an olive out of a dish and held it just in front of Vanessa's lips.

Vanessa bit into the olive and shrugged. "Just some people I don't really know."

s finds hope

Dan hailed a cab and opened the door for Serena. The October air was crisp and smelled of burnt sugar, and Dan suddenly felt very elegant and mature—a man in a tuxedo out on the town with a beautiful girl. He slid into the seat beside her and looked down at his hands as the cab pulled away from the curb. They weren't shaking anymore.

Unbelievable as it seemed, he had touched Serena with those very hands while they were dancing. And now he was alone with her in a taxi. If he wanted to, he could take her hand, stroke her cheek, maybe even kiss her. He studied her profile, her skin shining in the yellow glow of the streetlights, but he couldn't bring himself to do it.

"God I love to dance," Serena said, letting her head fall back on the seat. She felt completely relaxed. "I could seriously dance every single night."

Dan nodded. "Yeah, me too," he said. *But only with you*, he meant to add.

It takes a girl like Serena to make a guy with two left feet say he loves to dance.

They rode the rest of the way in silence, enjoying the tired feeling in their legs and the cool air from the open window on their sweat-dampened foreheads. There was nothing awkward about the fact that they weren't talking. It was nice.

When the cab pulled up in front of the old Barneys building on Seventeenth Street, Dan was expecting to see Jenny waiting for them outside, but the sidewalk was empty.

"I guess I'm going to have to go in there and get her," Dan said. He turned to Serena. "You can go ahead home. Or you can wait. . . ."

"I'll come with you," Serena said. "I may as well see what I missed out on."

Dan paid for the cab, and they got out and headed for the door.

"I hope they let us in," Serena whispered. "I threw my invitation out."

Dan pulled the crumpled invitation Jenny had made for him out of his pocket and flashed it at the bouncer at the door. "She's with me," he said, putting his arm around Serena.

"Go ahead," the bouncer said, waving them on.

She's with me? Dan couldn't believe his balls. He'd had no idea they were that big.

"I'd better look around for my sister," he told Serena when they got inside.

"Okay," she said. "I'll meet you back here in ten minutes."

The room was full of old familiar faces. So familiar that no one there was quite sure whether Serena van der Woodsen had just arrived or if she'd been there all night. She certainly looked like she'd been having a good time. Her hair was windblown, her dress was slipping off her shoulders, there was a run in her tights, and her cheeks were all pink, as if she'd been running. She looked wild, like the kind of girl who'd done everything everyone said she'd done, and probably a whole lot more.

Blair noticed Serena right away, standing on the edge of the dance floor in that funny old dress they'd bought together at Alice Underground.

Blair pulled away from Nate. "Look who's here," she said.

Nate turned around, gripping Blair's hand when he saw Serena, as if to demonstrate his devotion.

Blair squeezed his hand back. "Why don't you go tell her?" she asked him. "Tell her you can't be friends with her anymore." Her stomach rumbled nervously. After all the throwing up she'd done, she really needed another tuna roll.

Nate stared at Serena with grim, slightly stoned determination. If Blair thought it was crucial that he tell Serena to get lost, then he'd do it. He couldn't wait to get this all behind them so he could relax. In fact, after he talked to Serena he was going to head upstairs and find somewhere private to light up.

Waspoid rule #1: When things get intense, smoke a joint.

"All right," Nate said, letting go of Blair's hand. "Here I go."

"Hey," Serena said. She reached up and kissed Nate on the cheek. He blushed. He hadn't expected her to touch him. "You look mah-velous, darling," she said in a silly, hoity-toity accent.

"Thanks," Nate said. He tried to put his hands in his pockets, but his tuxedo didn't have any. Stupid thing. "So, what have you been up to?" he asked.

"Well, I kind of blew off the party," Serena explained. "I've been out dancing at this crazy place in Brooklyn."

Nate raised his eyebrows in surprise. But then again, nothing Serena said should have surprised him anymore.

"So, you want to dance?" Serena asked. She put her arms around Nate's neck before he answered, and began to swing her hips from side to side.

Nate glanced at Blair, who was watching them carefully, and

collected himself. "Look, Serena," he said, taking a step back and removing her arms. "I really can't . . . you know . . . be friends . . . not like the way we were before," he began.

Serena gazed into his eyes searchingly, trying to read his true thoughts. "What did I do?" she said. "Did I do something?"

"Blair is my girlfriend," Nate continued. "I have to . . . I have to be loyal to her. I can't . . . I can't really be . . ." He swallowed.

Serena crossed her arms over her chest. If only she could hate Nate for being so cruel and so lame. If only he weren't so good-looking. And if only she didn't love him.

"Well, I guess we should stop talking then," she said. "Blair might get mad." She let her arms fall to her sides and turned abruptly away.

As she crossed the room, Serena's eyes met Blair's. She stopped in her tracks and reached into her bag, searching for the twenty-dollar bill Blair had left on the table at the Tribeca Star. She wanted to give it back. As if, somehow, it would prove she hadn't done anything wrong. That night, or ever. Her fingers found her cigarettes instead. She pulled one out and stuck it between her lips. The music was getting louder and around her, people were dancing. Serena could feel Blair watching her, and her hands trembled as she fumbled around in her bag for a light. As usual, she didn't have one. She shook her head in annoyance, and glanced up at Blair. And then, instead of glaring at each other, the two girls smiled.

It was strange smile, and neither girl knew what the other meant by it.

Was Blair smiling because she had won the boy in the end and stamped all over Serena's party shoes? Because—as usual—she had gotten her way?

Was Serena smiling because she felt uncomfortable and nervous? Or was she smiling because she hadn't stooped to

Blair's petty level of spreading nasty rumors and playing with Nate's mind?

Or was it a sad smile because their friendship was over?

Maybe they were smiling because they both knew deep down that no matter what happened next—no matter what boy they fell in or out of love with, or what clothes they wore, or what their SAT scores were, or which college they got into—they both would be all right.

After all, the world they lived in took care of its own.

Serena pulled the cigarette out of her mouth, dropped it on the floor and began walking toward Blair. When they were face to face, she stopped and fished the twenty-dollar bill out of her bag. "Here," she said, handing it to Blair. "This is yours." And then, without another word, she kept on walking, heading for the ladies' room to splash some cold water on her face.

Blair looked down at the bill in her hand and stopped smiling.

Over by the door, Rebecca Agnelli from the Central Park Save the Peregrine Falcon Foundation was just putting on her mink coat and kissing Kati and Isabel goodnight. Blair walked over and pressed the twenty-dollar bill into her hand.

"That's for the birds," Blair said with her fakest smile. "Don't forget your gift bag!"

Serena turned on the tap and splashed her face over and over with cool clean water. It felt so good she wanted to peel off all her clothes and jump in.

She leaned against the row of sinks, patting her face dry. Her gaze slipped to the floor, where she saw a pair of black wing-tipped shoes, the fringed end of a blue scarf, and a girl's black handbag.

Serena rolled her eyes and walked over. "Chuck, is that

you?" she said into the crack in the door. "Who've you got in there with you?"

A girl gasped.

"Shit," Serena heard Chuck say.

Chuck had stood Jenny up on the toilet-seat lid in the end stall and pulled her dress down so he could get at those massive jugs. Serena had come at the worst possible time.

Chuck pushed open the stall door a few inches. "Fuck off," he growled.

Behind him Serena could see little Jenny Humphrey, her dress pulled down around her waist, her arms hugging herself, looking terrified.

Someone pushed open the bathroom door. "Jenny? Are you in here?" Dan called.

Serena suddenly registered: Jenny was Dan's sister. No wonder she'd sounded weird on the phone. She was about to be mauled by Chuck.

"I'm here," Jenny whimpered.

"Get out of here," Serena snapped at Chuck, pulling the door open just wide enough for him to get past her.

Chuck pushed by her, knocking her against the stall door. "Well, excuse me, bitch," he hissed. "Next time I'll be sure to ask your permission."

"Wait a minute, asshole," Dan said, sizing Chuck up. "What were you doing to my sister?"

Serena pushed the stall door closed and stood outside it, waiting for Jenny to step down from the toilet and fix herself before her brother saw her. Inside, she could hear Jenny sniffling.

"Fuck off," Chuck said, pushing Dan out of the way.

"No, you fuck off, Scarf Boy," Dan said. He'd never been in a fight before. His hands began to shake again.

Serena hated it when boys fought. It was so pointless, and it made them look like assholes.

"Hey Chuck," Serena said, poking Chuck in the back. Chuck turned around. "Why don't you go fuck yourself? You know no one else will," she hissed.

"You bitch," Chuck hissed back. "You think you can come back here and act all high and mighty after everything you've done? You think you can act like such a princess and tell *me* to fuck off?"

"What have I done, Chuck?" Serena demanded. "What is it that you think I've done?"

Chuck licked his lips and laughed quietly. "What have you done?" he asked. "You got kicked out of boarding school because you are a perverted slut who made marks on the wall above the bed in your dorm room for every boy you did. You have STDs. You were addicted to all kinds of drugs and busted out of rehab and now you're dealing your own stuff. You were a member of some cult that killed chickens. You have a fucking baby in France." Chuck took a deep breath and licked his lips.

Serena was smiling again.

"Wow. I've been busy," she said.

Chuck frowned. He glanced at Dan who was standing there, watching silently with his hands in his pockets.

"Fuck off, Chuck," Serena whispered.

Chuck shrugged and grabbed a bottle of Evian off the counter. "Whatever, bitch," he said, pushing past Dan and out the door.

"You know you love me!" Serena yelled after him.

Dan knocked on the bathroom stall. "Jenny?" he said gently. "Are you all right?"

More sniffling.

Jenny couldn't get control of herself. She just could not

believe that of all the people in the universe, it had to be Serena van der Woodsen who found her like this. Serena must think she was so pathetic.

"I'm okay," Jenny finally managed to say. She picked her purse up off the floor and pushed open the door. "Just take me home."

Dan put his arm around his sister and Serena took his hand. Together, they wound their way through the crowded party.

"Wait! Your gift bags!" Rain Hoffstetter squealed from her post at the front door. She handed Serena and Jenny each a black Kate Spade tote bag.

Dan pushed open the doors and ran out into the street to hail a cab. When he found one, Serena got in first, then Jenny, and then Dan. Jenny put her feet up on the hump in the floor and hugged her knees, resting her head against them. Serena reached down and stroked her curly brown hair.

"You guys go home first," Serena offered.

Dan glanced at Jenny. She needed to go to bed. "All right," he agreed, and gave the driver his address.

Serena leaned back, still stroking Jenny's hair. "Wow," she said ironically. "I haven't had this much excitement since I left boarding school."

Dan stared at her, his eyes wide and trusting. "So, those stories . . ." he said, and then he blushed. "I mean, did any of that happen, for real?"

Serena frowned. She fished in her bag for a cigarette, and then thought better of it. "Well, what do you think?" she asked.

Dan shrugged. "I think it's a bunch of bullshit," he said.

Serena raised her eyebrows playfully. "But how do you know for sure?" she asked.

Her mouth was open, the corners of it quavering up and

then down. Her blue eyes glowed in the light of a passing car.

No, Dan couldn't imagine her doing any of the things Chuck had accused her of. The only thing he could imagine her doing was kissing him. But there was time for that later.

"I just don't see you that way," he said.

The corners of Serena's mouth spread wide and she was smiling again.

"Good," she said. She took a deep breath and let her head fall back against the seat.

Dan let his head fall back beside hers. "Good," he agreed, closing his eyes.

As they sped past the flashing billboards and bright lights of Times Square, Serena kept her eyes open. She had always thought Times Square was ugly and depressing compared to the quiet, manicured streets of her neighborhood. But now the brilliant lights and loud noises and the steam rising from the grates on the corners gave her hope. In the darkness of the taxi, she reached for Dan's hand at the same moment he reached for hers.

She couldn't wait to see what would happen next.

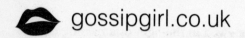

gossipgirl.co.uk

topics ◀ *previous*   *next* ▶   *post a question*   reply

Disclaimer: All the real names of places, people, and events have been altered or abbreviated to protect the innocent. Namely, me.

hey people!

Well, I had a great time at *Kiss on the Lips.* I must have lost fifteen pounds dancing—not that I needed to.

Needless to say, I'm feeling good.

Sightings

B and *N* going into his townhouse together late Friday night. *C* wandering down Tenth Avenue looking to get lucky with some Jersey girls. *D* and *J* and their scruffy dad eating a family break-fast on Saturday morning at that diner where they used to film **Seinfeld**. *V* renting horror moves with her new boyfriend in Brooklyn. *S* handing a black Kate Spade tote bag to a home-less man on the steps of the Met.

Your E-mail

 Hey GG,
Just wanted to tell you that I'm writing my college thesis on you. You rock!
—Studyboy

 Dear Studyboy,
I'm flattered. So . . . what do you look like?
—GG

QUESTIONS AND ANSWERS

Why worry about college? I'm having way too much fun right now. And there are so many questions to be answered:

Will **S** and **D** fall in love? Will **S** grow tired of his corduroys?

Will **J** swear off high society and fancy dresses and stick to friends her own age (even if they'll never be her bra size)?

Will **V** bust out and start wearing all sorts of bright colors? Will she grow her hair? Will she and that bartender get it on?

Will **B** stay with **N**?

Will **C** stop harassing young girls and admit that he's a loser?

Will **S** really make a movie? She's never even used a disposable Polaroid.

Will people stop talking about all of the above?

It's unlikely. I know I won't. It's all so good.

Until next time.

You know you love me,

gossip girl